IMMORAL DILEMMAS

made me feel a part of every story, every paragraph, every sentence. The writing pulled me in immediately, grabbed a hold of me with its disturbingly, blood saturated claws and did not let go, not even for a second, until it had wrung every last drop of horror and fear from my pores! It has fast become one of my fave collections ever!" —Corrina Morse, *NoRemorse Reviews*

"*Immoral Dilemmas* is a great collection of stories, deep and dreadful, written with precision and care for every blood-drenched detail. These thoughtful, terrifying tales will resonate long after reading them. Thomas Clark shows us yet again that he isn't fucking around." —Robert Essig, author of *This Damned House* and *Baby Fights*

"Horror, sex and violence bend the boundaries of reality and consciousness giving *Immoral Dilemmas* a distinguished Videodrome vibe." —Mike Rankin, *Horror Bookworm Reviews*

IMMORAL DILEMMAS

THOMAS R CLARK

NIGHTSWAN PRESS
Syracuse
—2023—

Nightswan Press
Syracuse, New York

www.thomasrclark.com

TABLE OF CONTENTS

FOREWORD
by Lisa Vasquez

It's a hit or miss for someone to take the time and read a foreword in a book. Still, being asked to write one is an amazing honor and I hope you take a moment to read this one.

I met Tommy in a whirlwind introduction at the Scares That Care convention in August of 2018. It was the end of the day, and he made his way to me among the scattered tables and littered floors. Scares is an experience in itself. Authors who have been lucky enough to attend talk about it all year until the next one. I was there with several authors from Stitched Smile Publications, and we were all exhausted from the amount of traffic and amazing conversations with readers. I think I was ready to crawl under the table and take a nap when he introduced himself. I'd seen and heard of him in our overlapping small circles, but we never formally met, until then.

Remember I said I was exhausted? Not this guy. He looked like he was getting a second wind and was about to do another shift. He handed me his book "Good Boy," his underground newsletter (which I still have) some bookmarks. We talked for a few minutes when he said, "I'd love for you to publish this book." Even with the crash of coming down from the day, my first impression of Tommy was how genuine he was (is). From that moment on, he and I have been through a friendship forged in heated, passionate debates and hysterical laughter.

Don't take that to mean his writing is all warm and fuzzy, though, as you'll see from the stories in this collection. I ended up publishing, "Good Boy" the following year and then later published "Bella's Boys" and "The Death List."

Since 2016, Stitched Smile's blog had what we called, "Stitched Saturday." Every week we'd throw out some writing prompts and invite authors to hone their skills. We posted their short stories on our blog for our readers to learn about the authors, follow them, and get mini samples of their work. Tommy was on every single one of them with the fervor of an obsessed writer. Later, we worked together on House of Stitched Magazine were Tommy had a featured series called, "Roots of Apathy" and touched on the contributions of Robert E. Howard, Clark Ashton Smith and August Derleth to the writing world.

What I loved most about working with Tommy, from mentoring him (for a fleeting moment, as that credit goes to Garrett) to watching his wings grow, putting him where he is now—an award-nominated author—is how grounded he is and how serious he takes his writing. Not only is he is always looking for ways to improve his craft and experiment with his range, but he is always humble in his acceptance of critique. This is why his work stands out.

It goes without saying, I believe in Tommy's talent as a writer.

Let me say this: Tommy's a tornado, and he will buzz around you like a swarm of bees. But somewhere in the middle of his energy and chaos is unfeigned warmth. He puts his soul and passion into every piece of work he places in your hand as if it's a personal gift he's crafted... because it is.

With this special collection, you're getting several of Tommy's best works from the spinning, dark waltz that is "*Dropping Karma*" to the nightmare version of America's iconic, favorite pastime (featuring a cameo appearance), "*For the Love of the Game.*" If you are new to Tommy's world, this collection will treat you to a glimpse of this author's diversity, and if you're a veteran fan, you'll appreciate having some of his best works in a single volume.

I've mentored and published many authors in my career, and Tommy is best in class. Why should you read his work? Because it's entertaining, it's authentic, and it's fucking brilliant. Once you step into his world, you'll be hooked because while you never know what he'll throw at you next, you'll take it like Chris Rock took that pimp hand.

Written in blood by the Queen's hand,

Lisa Vasquez

PART ONE
GHOSTS AREN'T SCARY...

DROPPING KARMA

Part One: The Drops

Things have been looking up for me since I promised to stop killing myself. I can't really say the same for everyone else. But me? I've been doing fine. Who I am isn't important. Hell, I've learned no names or designations are static. Why? Because everything changes.

Today I'm sitting on a stool at a diner, staring at my reflection in the mirror behind the counter. I haven't seen myself in a few years and, all vanity aside, I'm happy with my appearance. I better be, it's about as good as it's ever going to get.

My hair is long, and dark, with a few streaks of silver and white. The gray makes me look wiser and more distinguished than I am, while piercing hazel eyes stare back at me, hiding secrets better left untold.

The man sitting two stools down wears a postal uniform. He's eating a piece of cherry pie and it's evident he likes it. He's cutting off more than he should and shoveling it into his mouth. The red sauce drips off his fork, trailing down his chin, and splatters as it lands on the counter.

He snorts as he wolfs down the dessert and wipes off his chin with a napkin. A waitress hands him more napkins, then stops in front of me, blocking my view of the mirror. The server, a blue-haired, frumpy matron in a plain smock, offers me coffee. I forgo the brew, asking for cold water instead. She happily obliges.

As the waitress pours the water into my glass, I watch the ice swirl about in the self-contained maelstrom. The cubes of frozen water clink off the surface and chaos reigns as a battle between gravity and buoyancy is fought. She stops when it is full, and soon order prevails. The water settles, the ice floats to the top, and all is tranquil and calm.

I sip from a straw, taking care not to disturb the new found serenity within the confines of the tumbler. The water is cold and crisp, and I feel a bit of ecstasy as I swallow. It's euphoric and somewhat familiar, a mirror of my life as of late.

It's a bitch to break an addiction of this magnitude. Personal experience has taught me how one could abuse the fuck out of it. I'm happy now, I think. For the past seven years or so, abstinence has been working out for me.

I didn't ask for this curse, but multiple lapses in judgment have led me to this juncture, and I'll own all of them. Once you learn how to drop, it's easy to damn yourself to some form of Hell.

Shit, I'm only now learning stopping doesn't prevent you from paying the tithe for a previous infraction or stop others from dragging you along with them on a drop. According to science, for every action, there is an equal and opposite reaction, right? I accepted this, but I never anticipated how the side effects of breaking the cycle might affect others.

The cold ice in the tumbler is a stark reminder of the first time I dropped-well, the first time I can remember dropping. I see it in the glass, reflecting back, reminding me of the fractured being I've become. I watch it unfold, as I do with all of my dreams, as an outsider.

The girl's hands shoot forward as she runs, hitting the frosted storm door of the porch. The metal door on the little white house flies open with a loud crack, resonating through the chill air of the early winter evening. The girl bursts through the threshold, bundled for the weather in appropriate attire, sans the overlarge boots she wears.

Her father's boots.

They are far too big for her little feet, but she doesn't care. It isn't everyday Mom lets her get the mail, and in her excited haste, she instead slipped her father's boots on. The child perseveres in her quest and jumps, bounding past the four steps connecting the porch to the sidewalk and driveway.

Landing with a grunt, she expels her breath, creating a fog of ice crystals in the crisp air. Tiny feet slide in the boots, and she wavers, almost toppling over. Regaining her balance, the girl's eyes attempt to adjust to the twilight of dusk and three-foot high snow banks obscuring her destination.

The mailbox across the street.

Orientating herself, the girl strikes forward without further hesitation. She half slides, half runs down the expanse of the driveway, dodging ice patches and lumps of snow.

A dozen and a half strides later the girl reaches the driveway's end, and the road. With her goal in view, she stops, not forgetting her mother's last words as she suited up, "Look both ways before you cross the road, young lady!"

Doing as her mother said, she peers left and then right, and left, again. Seeing no vehicles or headlights, she decides to traverse the salted tarmac and lunges forward. She is half way across when the world lights up, telling her something has gone horribly wrong.

And this is where things get fucked. Because I remember it all as if it happened at this moment. A small hill universally hid me and the driver from one another. I didn't see the car coming. The driver, an old woman, simply forgot to turn on her headlights in the dim light.

She accelerated as she ascended, hitting some forty-five miles per hour. At this point she realized her lights were off. She took her eyes off the road for a moment and turned them on, flooding the road and illuminating me, who was committed to my ill-fated actions.

I turned to see the Buick's lights upon me as time slowed to nothing. The woman looked up, saw me with my eyes open wide, and slammed on her brakes. The laws of physics took control from here, a catalyst for all to come, or so I once believed.

She struck me in place and watched in terror as my body

crumpled onto the hood of the vehicle. My midsection and ribs were crushed. I felt no pain.

I moved in slow motion, my broken body bounced off the hood of the car. My head slammed into the windshield and popped like a melon, shattering the safety glass, covering it in pink and red. Inertia carried my body over the car, somersaulting it to the road behind the vehicle with an audible plop. The brakes and tires squealed as rubber caught the pavement and the car finally stopped.

I fucking died. I experienced it, through every horrible moment of the collision. The car mangled my body into a pulpy corpse.

The old woman exits the Buick and finds a pair of boots, standing up as if they had been placed there. In the snowbank directly in front of her is the girl, her stocking feet sticking out of the snow bank, her body wiggling to fight free of the dirty snow and ice. She is cold, half buried in the snow. She feels a tug on her backside as she is pulled out. The night is lit up by the headlights of a car.

"Oh, thank God you're alive!" The girl hears the strange woman say.

"What happened?" She asks, shocked, staring in awe at the car, her boots, and the woman.

"Oh, my God. Oh, no!" The girl hears her mother, hysterically screaming, as she runs down the driveway.

"What happened?" The girl asks.

"Why did you do that, young lady?" The woman driving the car exclaims.

"Huh?" The girl replies, not understanding what is going on. She has no idea how she got in the snowbank; let alone why she is outside. Her mother reaches them at this point, tears streaming down her face. She grabs the girl and holds her tight.

"I told you to look both ways!"

The three people stand in the cold winter night, lit by the red and white lights. A fog grows in the wake of the car's exhaust, the sick sweet smell of salt and carbon monoxide tinges the air.

"Your daughter is awfully lucky, ma'am," the lady says, "it wasn't her time to go, that much is obvious."

But I did die, *the girl thinks.*

Her mother holds the girl in a death-grip hug and sobs into her bosom, unaware of her daughter's paradox.

The nightmares came next. Through a forest nestled deep within the recesses of my mind, a girl ran, jumping over logs and dodging brambles. She dared not stop. She knew what chased her. She knew it would never stop, not until it caught the girl, and thus she ran as fast as her small legs could carry her. Her breath labored; her heart pounded in her chest. Her legs ached with burning fire, but she knew if she stopped, it would fucking kill her.

A great vacuum came to life, sucking everything out of the forest. Darkness erupted and filled the girl's world with shadow while she tumbled with the rest of the debris into the void.

The nightmare ended and a new one began. Bright lights flooded the dream in a brilliant, white sheet.

Memories of an accident that didn't happen sped through on fast forward as a car hit the girl.

The girl wakes up.

Too terrified to cry out, I violently shook my head to make the lingering visions of my death go away. And it worked. Each time I shook, it blissfully removed the images from my memory until the next time I would close my eyes to sleep.

The nightmares continued until I became numb to them. In time, what remained of these visions became a blur of soothing imagery, calming me. I all but forgot the night terrors as I grew into a woman.

I smile and suck down my drink. The water is refreshing, yet also a trigger for another of my repressed memories from my tenth birthday, five years later. Doctors claim all of my drops are, and I quote, *"A product of an overactive imagination, concocted as a coping device from some trauma event."* They're right about the latter, but there's nothing imaginary about a drop. They're all too real.

The weekly family get-togethers at her Aunt and Uncle's lake house are joyous occasions. The late summer is always best, not so hot or buggy, and this day is no different. The air is thick with the delicious smells of a Yankee clam bake. Steamed little neck clams, hamburgers, hotdogs, melted butter, peppers, onions and sausages. Don't forget the salt potatoes, and Grandma Brown's baked beans.

The adults sit around a fire pit drinking their beverages of choice as the girl and her cousins play hide-n-seek in the garage and the thick grove of evergreens encircling the property. All is well.

The girl works up a sweat playing and insists on going swimming in the lake.

"Don't go out over your head," her mother warns.

"I won't!" the girl replies. Without further hesitation, she runs down the stony driveway to the wooden dock, kicks off her flip flops and dives into the warm lake water.

Though her mother and father warned her about going too far out, over her head, the girl did anyway. Unaware of its strength, the current catches her and pulls her out further. By the time she realizes it is too late. Her toes fail to touch the bottom with her head above water, and she panics. Flailing her arms about, screaming for help, she swallows gulps of lake water.

I drowned. Agonizing, liquid fire filled my lungs and I felt bitterly cold, as if ice poured down my throat. Bright lights assailed my eyes, blinding me, adding to the chaos as I kicked my feet, trying desperately to reach the shore. But the undercurrent kept pulling me back. Then I felt the weight of the water drag me down.

The adults heard my screams from the yard. My mother cried out and my father bolted down the hill. He streaked across the dock and dove in. By then I stopped fighting, too tired to do anything other than embrace the bliss of drowning overcame me. I opened my eyes and saw a distorted reflection of myself there in the water, standing above me. My face distorted and morphed into a man's face, my father's. Then I died.

He reached his daughter too late.

A hand pulls the girl up and out of the water. She takes a deep breath, relishing the fresh air, gulping it as water spills out of her mouth.

She looks to his rescuer. It is her father.

"Are you okay?" The girl's father asks her. The girl nods and her father, relieved his daughter is safe, carries the girl to the shore where her mother waits.

"I told you not to go out over your head!" Her mother says, shaming her.

It's the little Mandela Effects, the changes when you drop, I find are the most aggravating. Being more cognizant of life in general at ten years of age, I started noticing them after this drop. They're little things, like the spelling of a name, changing Lori to Lauri, or the colors in an advertisement. Sometimes it's the jingle of a product. Or, my personal favorite, when the actor on a television show I watched every day suddenly became a different actor all together with the same name.

My family would laugh, tell me I was making it up. But I knew something changed when I dropped after dying. When it happened to my boyfriend, after he let me borrow his bike, I finally caught on. His name changed. Everything else about him was the same. But his fucking name.

—

The young girl is now a teenager, riding her boyfriend's bicycle. He lives a few towns away, an hour's ride on the bike, and the teenager enjoys long rides. The road is lined with low elevation hills, barely noticeable unless you happen to be pedaling up one.

The teenager hits the top of a slope, throws her hands into the air, and crosses the highway, letting inertia pull her down. Her balance keeps the bike from tipping over.

It doesn't allow her to turn from the path of the oncoming car.

Hidden by the hill, a yellow and black Grand Prix swoops at her, an unforgiving juggernaut of steel and glass. The teenager experiences a schism in time, she knows she is pedaling, but the bike stays in place until she pushes her legs to move. The driver's face is hidden by the glare of the sun on the windshield. She drops her hands back to the handlebars and makes a vain attempt to steer the bicycle away.

She almost makes it.

The car clips the back tire and catapults the teenager off the bike.

Tumbling through the air, I watched the mile marker grow closer with each moment. The car flipped over multiple times, ejecting the driver through the window. Then time caught back up with me in a breath. The flipped car's faux-leather roof landed on top of its driver, squishing his guts out his mouth like a toad.

I landed ass first on the mile marker and felt it skewer me, entering my body through the posterior. Physics drove my body down, allowing the steel post to pass through my internal organs, enter my neck, and subsequently push my brains out the new hole in the top of my head. Vlad Tepes would have likely been unhappy with my self-impalement.

I didn't suffer enough.

The driver squeals on the Grand Prix's brakes, leaving a black trail of rubber behind it. The teenager tucks and rolls as she hits the pavement and rolls away from the oncoming car. It barely misses her. The girl comes to rest next to a mile marker post.

The teenager sits up and shakes the bits of gravel and sand off her person. The driver, a man, is disheveled and harrowed from the experience. He wears a t-shirt featuring an old-timey pro-wrestler, the American Hope.

"Are you okay? I almost killed you," he asks, his voice shaking.

Maybe you did, *the teenager who was once a young girl thinks to herself.*

And my boyfriend? Whose name mysteriously changed? For some reason, he didn't get upset at all over his bike getting smashed in. This is when I figured it out. At least I thought I did. It's also when I started calling these reality shifts "drops," like I'm dropping into another life. There's no time travel, no reincarnation involved. You simply carry on as if nothing ill happened. You might still get hit by the car, but you don't die or suffer serious injury, at least in my experiences.

Science says you need to verify experiments for it to be true, right? Let's say the laboratory results led me to grow reckless after my epiphany, unveiling this new parlor trick. Teenage me, and her budding sexuality, discovered something she loved about it.

It turned me on.

Outside a tractor trailer buzzes by, blaring on its air

horn. I sip on my water and smile. I'm reminded of my first time, and of the boy whose name, and so much more, changed.

Her boyfriend receives a car for his birthday, a Chevrolet Chevette. After the drive-in and a new movie starring Sinbad as a genie, they are out joyriding, cruising the country roads. Though she doesn't have a license, her fellation skills are persuasive, and he lets her drive anyhow.

They speed down a dark back road, straight for miles, allowing her to red-line the subcompact car's speedometer. An intersection approaches, and down this side road rests their destination, a regional cemetery the local kids use as a make-out spot.

She sees a pair of headlights in the distance and guesses she'll have enough time to make the turn before the oncoming vehicle reaches the intersection.

The tractor trailer, a huge, red Big Mack truck, rolls down the road. The truck driver utilizes the back road as an alternate route slow with traffic, or state police. He cruises along at seventy-five miles an hour, bending the speed limit by ten. When the dots of the small car's headlights appear, he doesn't have a reason to believe the car will attempt to make a left turn in front of him.

But it did.

I might have been able to make it if my boyfriend hadn't grabbed the wheel of the Chevette in his own panic. A microsecond of distraction, and when it happened, the driver couldn't brake.

The rig smashed into the side of the subcompact car. The truck's logo, a bulldog in a pose with the words BIG MACK, smashed into my boyfriend's face.

Pieces of metal, glass and plastic erupted onto the highway. The truck's brakes squealed, sliding the tires across with a high piercing scream, as the driver attempted to stop her vehicle. The trailer flipped, catching the pieces of the small car in its wake, scraping and plowing them together.

Inside the car, I watched as my boyfriend and I amalgamated into a flesh and bone cornucopia. The initial impact drove him into me, crashing our upper bodies together into a blood and bone omelet. Before the lights turned to darkness, I noticed his pelvis and legs were at eye-level with our heads.

The Mack truck whizzes by, shaking the sub compact.

"Pull over, I'm driving. You're grounded from my car, chick."

"As long as I'm not grounded from you, that's all that matters," she reaches over and gropes him, turned on by the life and death experience.

"That can be arranged if you keep pulling this kind of shit," he protests. His cock stirs and comes to life as the teenage girl continues to fondle him. Pheromones fill the car's cab.

"Oh, come on, where is your sense of excitement?"

"Don't you ever do that again!" The boy tears the keys out of the teenage girl's hand.

"We're alive, aren't we?" She says.

"Barely!" He replies. The two switch seats. He takes over the

wheel of the car and they arrive at their destination, the county cemetery.

She's euphoric, her heart throbs in her chest, anticipating the inevitable. The couple slinks behind a mausoleum and explores each other's bodies. She lays upon a sarcophagus like a sacrificial offering. He climbs on top, her legs spread. With a hand, she guides him into her. She'll never forget this, the sting of her first time. Soon, blood and discharge from the act covers the granite, a sacrament completing the ritual.

I smile at these memories of love and teenage lust and wonder what became of the boyfriend. I doubt I'll ever know. But I do know, when the Big Mack—

—*Mack truck, Mack. Truck. Not Big Mack,* I remind myself and sip on my water.

When the Mack truck hit us, and I dropped, more things changed. It started when the nightmares from my youth returned, and my luck took a turn for the worst. The dense forest, the girl running through its murky depths, and the whirlwind sucking everything into a void. It all tormented me until I remembered how to subdue it, shaking it from my head when the visions lingered into my waking hours.

Controlling the nightmares didn't stop life from shitting on me. The boyfriend dumped me. We argued over the movie we saw the night I let him take my cherry, he claimed the movie wasn't real. Then, during the make-up sex, I called him by the old name I knew him as from the previous drop. He accused me of sleeping around on him, questioning the identity of this person and where he could find him.

I told him the truth, about dying and dropping and all the batshit crazy accompanying it. But he wouldn't hear any more lunacy from me, as he called it.

I flunked out of college, next. I found I would have trouble keeping jobs for some reason. My life tumbled into a downward spiral of one bullshit thing after another. Twice I found myself forced to trade sex for a month's rent.

A few pregnancy scares and wondering how I'd feed two mouths led to a couple outpatient visits at Planned Parenthood. Each visit left me numb. The clacking of the suction hose's air pump resonated in my memory. The earworm carried into my dreams, enhancing the soundtrack of the nightmares of old.

The last time, I went home and held a razor blade over my forearm for two hours before setting it down.

"How in the fuck can I kill myself for real?" I asked myself, "I can't!" I screamed and threw the razor. It stuck in the wall. I made a promise to myself on this day to never drop of my own accord again, fearing more drops would lead to more bad shit.

I decided I'd learned a valuable lesson from my mistakes. The days of me instrumenting my own demise for the thrill of it saw their time in the limelight. I now knew the true ramifications, the cause and effect of killing yourself. I made my bed and accepted the consequences.

I blocked out the dreams. I adapted to the understanding the little things in life would go wrong for me and to expect it. I resolved to stay the course and carry on. I dealt myself this hand, and an adult deals with it and perseveres.

I didn't choose to drop again and avoided circumstances where I'd have to best as I could. It lasted until the next Easter at the mall. I fucking hate Easter, now and haven't celebrated since. It's ironic, considering the holiday's message of death and rebirth.

"May I?" I ask the waitress as she walks by, tipping my glass at her. She nods and refills it.

"You new around here? Passing through?" She asks me.

"Yes, and no, actually," I reply, "I'm waiting for someone, truth be told."

"Of course, you are," she winks at me and returns to her duties behind the counter.

The young woman who was once a girl makes a stripped-down fashion statement, wearing a white t-shirt, jeans and sneakers to the mall. She peers over the railing on the fourth floor of the atrium, overlooking the commons.

Five stories below her stands a pink mall Easter Bunny, all seven feet of him, from the tips of his ears to his toes. The rabbit's assistants are taking photographs with the families of mall shoppers. Pastel neon lights surround the Easter Bunny's artificial lair. Standing in line to greet the holiday mascot is a menagerie of children and their parents.

The woman who was once a girl is perplexed, she feels a chill, as cold as a midwinter day. She turns away and seeks the elevator, passing a storefront on the way and sees the Easter Bunny run by. How can this be? The Bunny is downstairs, four floors, hippity hopping as the line of children snaked away from his lair.

The woman is distracted from the thought by the shrill bell heralding the elevator's arrival. The stainless-steel doors reflect back, and she sees the Easter Bunny, once again.

Sixty seconds of terror came next. I stepped on board. The convex elevator car's huge Lexan panels provided me with an unobstructed view of the mall. Through these windows, I saw the Easter Bunny in the reflection of the glass.

Something went wrong with the elevator car. It lurched and dropped. I felt the elevator descend, then it stopped and jerked. The people below me, frantic as they watched the car's cables malfunction, ran in all directions. I heard the high-tension cables snap and crack like a whip. Everyone ran from the imminent disaster, except the Easter Bunny, who stood frozen in place.

I slid toward the glass and my hands shot forward, catching the metal handrail encircling the elevator car's interior. A horrible squealing erupted, and the car tipped at a forty-five degree angle, dropping further. I held on to the rail. My weight shifted the balance of the car, causing the elevator to creak and bend.

Until it fell.

The car plummeted three stories down. People screamed and scattered. I watched as the floor rushed impossibly fast at my face.

The Easter Bunny watched, too.

Lights glared and flashed, the world crashed around me as the car creaked, tipped and fell to the floor of the mall commons. Metal, glass, and body parts are strewn about. I watched the floor rush at me. Then it stopped. A pool of crimson blood formed at the Easter Bunny's feet, pooling out from my point of impact. The Easter Bunny reached out to me with a pair of white gloved hands.

"Fuck you, Easter Bunny," I said before I died.

The young woman who was once a girl hesitates, then turns from the elevator. She decides to take an alternate route. She sees the Easter Bunny far below. The seven-foot-tall pink monstrosity beckons her with white gloved hands.

"Fuck you, Easter Bunny," she says as she walks away.

She hears the car crimple and fall. But she's not onboard. Screams and shouting erupt from the chaos of the disaster, and she doesn't look back. She doesn't need to witness the carnage. Instead, her focus is on her own reflection in the window of a mall shop.

At first, the young woman does not recognize the person. It is a young man wearing the clothes she put on this morning, a pair of jeans and a t-shirt.

She looks down her shirt and sees the chest of a man. Pilling on the waist of the jeans, she sees her panties have been replaced by boxers.

All in three footsteps.

She understands what has happened.

I stared, not fully comprehending the outcome of the drop. Names changing, movies disappearing, eyes and hair taking up new colors. But my sex?

My memories told me I grew up a girl, but the person standing before me in the mirror was a man. Body and gender dysphoria set in as the hormonal cocktail in my body shifted a chromosome.

I ran home and hid in my apartment for a week, afraid to go out. As the days passed, my memories settled and melded into one. More shocking things came to be in the wake of the drop.

My luck… got better. An unexpected windfall of opportunities came my way. Apparently, the me from this reality misfiled my taxes years prior and received a five-digit settlement check from the IRS.

As I adjusted to my body, as much as I missed being 'me,' I promised to hold to my convictions and never drop of my own accord. I couldn't be sure if I would shift back to being a woman.

As a result, for six more years I lived as a man. I took a new job as an over the road trucker and worked in tandem on long hauls with a driving partner. And, as if fate would have it any other way, we drove a big, red Mack truck.

The young man who was once a girl is sleeping in the bunk of a tractor trailer. His partner is behind the wheel, and this night, he too is sleeping, though he shouldn't be. His unmedicated diabetes has caused him to have a narcoleptic moment. And now, without the driver to regulate its speed; the truck, hauling a full payload of grocery items, is a forty-ton juggernaut barreling down the highway.

The road comes to a construction zone. The man who was

once a girl is still oblivious to the danger his co-worker has placed them in. The truck hits a grated bump, jarring the driver to his senses.

The driver wakes, startled, to find a sea of taillights before him as the lanes narrow to a single path lined with luminescent orange cones.

Sleeping in the bunk, at first, I believed it all to be part of a dream. I didn't know my co-worker over compensated and slammed on the Mack truck's brakes, causing a lethal chain reaction on the highway. The trailer jack-knifed as the semi burned rubber into the grooved pavement.

The thirty-five-foot-long trailer cleared a swath through the cones into oncoming traffic. The trailer hit a tanker truck with a full load of gasoline first. The tank flipped in response.

Inside the cab, the screeching of metal and my partner screaming to God woke me up in time to look out the window and see the tanker trailer flipping on its side. It cut into the cones before connecting with a trio of sedans and exploding. Fire rained down on everything in its vicinity. My nightmare became reality.

The impact threw me out of the bunk and into the cab. I'm spared the horror of being burned alive, instead I'm ejected through the windshield. I landed on the road next to a school bus. In the moments before a car slammed into the bus and crushed me, I watched a ball of fire erupt in the cab. The flames covered him, blistering and melting his skin and vaporizing his hair.

"I'm on fire!" I could hear him scream before the spreading flames burned the oxygen in his lungs and engulfed the remainder of the tractor's cab.

A microsecond later, the bus and a KIA Soul sandwiched me. I remember noticing a difference in the timbre of metal bending and the crack of bone breaking, before the vehicles crushed my skull. The kids in the bus were treated to a full view of my head exploding before they, too, were incinerated in the fireball.

The man who was once a girl sits straight up in the bunk of the truck, banging his head on the roof. He pats around his body until he realizes he is fine. Covered in a sheen of sweat, the rivulets drip down his face, stinging his eyes.

"You okay up there?" His partner asks.

"Yeah, I'm fine. Just a nightmare. How about you?" His voice is higher pitched than normal, and he resolves he needs a drink of water. He rubs the knot on his forehead from the blow and looks out the small window of the bunk. The brakes and headlights of cars traveling on the highway send pulsing lasers in flashes of brilliance into the cab's interior. Then he notices his face… has changed.

"I'm doing great, we'll be home in two hours. Got a construction zone coming up, but after that, smooth sailing. Go back to bed, you need the sleep."

The man who was once a girl isn't listening to the driver. He's discovering he is now the she he once was…

I still believed a legitimate, albeit vivid nightmare played out while I slept until I saw my reflection in the window.

I slid my hand down my pants to itch my balls, but instead found a familiar vulva I've not felt in over half a decade.

If you think this shocked me, it did. But my co-worker? He acted as if I were a woman all along. But he did notice something.

"I thought your eyes were brown," he said to me when we reached the hub.

"Why? What color are they now?"

"Hazel, on the green side."

I shrugged my shoulders and said I never noticed, must be a puberty thing and parted ways. I should have been more alert to what transpired.

I discovered the karma you dropped between realities has a way of catching up with you. Those pieces of yourself you leave behind? They find their way back. It's how you deal with them that either damns or defines you.

For me, I learned to deal with the side effects. Other people, as it turns out, didn't have as thick of skin. Like my driving partner, for example. I learned he became fraught with nightmares of his own. He refused to let me know what they were about, alleging he forgot them as he woke.

I knew better. I shared an intimate relationship with my own versions of the nightmares terrifying him as he slept. But whereas I developed coping mechanisms to deal with the memories of dying from an early age, he did not.

One morning his wife called me, distraught.

"He woke up in bed screaming 'I'm on fire!' over and over again!" She said, tears streaming down her face. I promised her I would talk to him, and I did. I tried letting him know I understood his dilemma and the nightmares. He wouldn't listen. After all, how could I know what went on in his head?

A week later I went into work and learned his wife found him dead over the weekend.

"I told him not to buy that damn gun and insisted he didn't need it. But being an over the road trucker, he justified the purchase." She said to me at the funeral. I found myself bitter at the irony in a weapon purchased for self-defense being used as a device for self-euthanasia.

I blamed the drops, not him. To take your own life, a person's brain must be broken in some manner to overcome their sense of self-preservation. Dropping will break your mind. It will shatter you and take pieces from you.

Typical of suicides, he did leave a note, a riddle with no explanation for his choice to take his own life.

"Now I'm whole again," is all it said.

His other friends and family didn't understand his cryptic words, but I knew the answer. When you drop, a part of you remains in the life you left behind. You become fractured, losing bits like memories and those damn Mandela Effects. You learn to cope, to live with the lost memories or the little nuances of change. Or you go batshit.

Up until recently, I didn't believe the pieces could be put back together. My co-worker believed he solved the puzzle, too, in his madness at the end. All you have to do is stop the cycle and let the pieces catch up. He did it the only way he knew how.

With gunpowder and lead.

Did he drop, again? Probably, and once you are aware of dropping, you'll likely never forget them. They'll stack up, as time shortens between each incident. The circumstances surrounding the drop play a key role. In life, karma catches up with you sooner or later, but when you drop, its effects are more immediate. The more you drop, the more you risk entering an eternity of squeezing a trigger or cutting a vein. Or worse.

I didn't want to think about what a constant stream of suicides would resemble. Hell is the only thing I can think of to describe this. It's why I stopped killing myself in the first place. The fear of this damnation.

I look at the clock on the wall. It's three o'clock. A familiar minivan pulls into the parking lot of the diner, right on time. A few moments later, he comes inside and sits at a private table. I sip down the rest of my water, retrieve a wad of bills from my purse, and set them on the counter. It's a generous tip for the waitress.

"Didn't you say you were meeting someone here?"

"I did," I answer, nod, excuse myself, and leave. The bells hanging off the door jingle as it closes behind me.

Part Two: Karma

I wait in my SUV near the rear of the parking lot for him to finish his meal. Eventually he exits the diner and drives away. As I follow him into the rural hills outside the city, my mind drifts back. I remember the days leading up to now.

Soon after my co-worker's suicide, a school shooting made the news. Complete with a body count straight out of a Japanese manga, other similar events paled in comparison.

When the report of the tragedy broke, I didn't understand its relevance to me. Why would I see any connection between a random school shooting and a multi-vehicle accident from my nightmares? Typically, I wouldn't. I didn't find the shooter's death by cop at the scene to be surprising, either. But when the news revealed him to be an unemployed oil company truck driver, it caught my attention.

His picture, broadcast on televisions, brought a sensation of Deja Vu to me. I'd seen this man somewhere before, at least I believed I did. Then, a memorial video to the dozens of victims at the massacre aired. I knew the faces of these children, too. I saw them in my nightmares, staring down at me from the windows of a bus.

"It's like their deaths are catching up with them," I said in a moment of epiphany. *What happened to the rest of them*, I postulated in thought, *the others who survived my drops and were blissfully unaware?* What has become of them since I stopped dropping and karma caught up with the lot of us?

As I recalled the drops I am conscious of, and the number of people involved in each, a realization overcame me.

They're all in danger of the same fate as my lover.

Each of them is no different from the kids in the school, and the truck driver who has now killed them twice.

The lady who knocked me out of my father's boots with her Buick remained a family friend until her death from being old, a couple years later.

A decade after, my father died from ass cancer, and dementia took its hold on my mother. She's still doing the two-slipper shuffle in the psych ward of the state hospital. This left a short list of people to track down. It included an ex-boyfriend, a truck driver, a pro-wrestling journalist, and the fucking Easter Bunny.

The last proved to be the easiest to find, the sorry son of a bitch tasked with wearing the Easter Bunny suit. A springtime trip to the mall later, I stood in line with families waiting to have their picture taken with the holiday effigy.

The Easter Bunny noticed me behind a family of six. He stepped away, out of sight, unannounced to his helpers. The line came to a stop as people searched for the anthropomorphic mascot. Photography assistants hung a sign declaring the Easter Bunny would be back in fifteen minutes.

How can you lose a seven-foot-tall fucking cartoon character? I wondered. A woman's scream from afar answered my question moments later. I turned to the sound in time to see the Easter Bunny face plant from a seven story hop down the mall's central atrium rabbit hole.

The head piece rolled off the body on impact, leaving a crimson streak behind it. The smiling face came to a stop at my feet, grinning at me with its buck-toothed mouth.

Next to me, the family of six's little ones cried hysterically, turning away from the scene. They came here expecting to get their pictures taken with the Easter Bunny. This happened, but not in a manner their parents would have hoped for. Instead, the kids were gifted with a post-traumatic stress imprint, courtesy of a decapitated costume still containing the actor's head.

Thoughts of how and why the Easter Bunny took off ran through my mind. Like, *Why did he run and jump when he saw me? Did my presence trigger something, causing him to snap?* I walked away, disappointed, not wanting to talk to authorities or be a part of what would surely become a media circus event.

I learned later his co-workers heard him repeating the Humpty Dumpty nursery rhyme as he slipped away.

"Humpty Dumpty sat on a wall
Humpty Dumpty had a great fall

*All the king's horses and all the king's men
Couldn't make Humpty whole again…"*

Tracking down the wrestling journalist turned out to be easier than I first thought. Recalling the t-shirt he wore, for the American Hope, I searched the internet and found a video on YouTube. It featured the aforementioned wrestler in an alleged interview hosted by my mark.

Social media told me he would be at a regional independent show on a specific date. I bought a ticket online. As I drove up to the parking lot of the American Legion, a sign advertising 'WREST ING THIS SUNDAY' loomed over the line of fans stretched around the side of the building. I wondered what happened. Did the 'L' simply fall off the signage, or hadn't they bothered, and left an empty space? Did it have an 'L' in another reality?

The interior reeked of stale draft beer, rotten feet, and ass funk. The promoters squeezed as many chairs as they could into the event. Fans stood elbow to blowhole, and more than once some unseen hand fondled my ass or grabbed a tit. I endured the first half of the show from the GA bleachers; sitting between a few unique characters. To my left, a couple in matching satin jackets cheered on the heels. On the right, a brood of Mennonites, a family of at least an Amish baker's dozen, spread out in a crescent surrounding me.

At half-time, I found the journalist outside smoking. The sight of me gave him pause. At first, he tried ignoring me, pretending not to recognize the face from his nightmares, but his body language betrayed his deception. In an effort to avoid talking, he stepped too close to a flood light and a haze of bugs freaked him out.

"You know, I've seen what it does to people," he said, breaking his silence and swatting at the insects.

"What is that?" I asked him.

"Hell, of course. I know what it is, and I won't go there," he said, "I can't shake the nightmares from my head. I can't help but keep thinking, *part of me was left behind and I need to be whole again.*" Without another word, he ran off, hopped into his car, the same Grand Prix from a decade ago- only a bit more rusted and burning oil, and drove away.

I followed in my SUV. I couldn't have been more than a few minutes behind him, but in a city, a few minutes is a lifetime. My phone rang, distracting me from the road. The number came up as unknown on my caller ID. In my peripheral I saw the mark's car at a stop light to my left. I sent the call to voicemail as I cut hard on the wheel.

The light turned green, and the race started. He sped off and found an onramp to the interstate. I followed and could see the red of his taillights rocketing away down the highway. I floored the gas pedal in pursuit, but his lights still disappeared on the horizon.

Five minutes later, halfway across a railyard bridge, I came upon his rusted-out, old Grand Prix pulled off on the shoulder. As I got closer, I noticed a shape standing on the roof. The journalist jumped as I whizzed by.

I jammed on the brakes. The tires squealed on the

blacktop, leaving a streak of burned rubber in my wake. A three point turn later, my SUV rolled back up the bridge and stopped next to his. I threw the door open and peered over the edge of the railing. A hundred feet below, his body lay splayed out on the tracks. Stunned, I watched as a train, engine horn blaring, struck his body. If the fall didn't kill him, the train's ability to transform a living being into ground beef did.

I drove home, discouraged, before the emergency vehicles and police arrived. With my mind focused on not one, but two people jumping to their deaths after crossing paths with me, I went straight to bed. I felt I deserved the pass, which I did earn. But in doing so, I forgot to check my phone's voicemail.

"You can might've all day long, but in the end, might've doesn't get the job done," I say aloud, still following the man in his car. He pulls down a country road near a large lake. I switch off my headlights and make sure he doesn't see me follow. My goal is to save lives, not watch another person jump to their death, or worse. Each time one of the doomed has seen me, they've gone off the deep end, literally. Their blood is on my hands. I pull off to the side of the road, watching the trucker's property from around a bend.

It's a rickety shanty, and part of me wonders how someone can live in such conditions. The stench of the place drifts on the wind. Sickly sweet and reeking of death, it makes me nauseous. The caution leading me to this point came in the form of the message left in my voice mail the night the journalist took the

A-train. I forgot the call came, and as a result, I didn't listen to it until late the next morning.

"Hi, it's Mom. Call me when you get this message. I had the nightmare again last night. You know when you were born, abortion laws weren't what they are today, and I had thought about getting one. I even went to the clinic, but I walked out. But in my nightmare, I didn't, I stayed and went through with it. Something must have gone wrong, because in my nightmare, after the procedure, I hemorrhaged, and bled to death on the operating table. It's a nightmare, but it's so vivid, like it happened."

Maybe it did, Mom, I thought to myself as I called her back. The call went straight to voicemail. I left before the beep, running to my car and driving to the nursing home.

The visions of the girl in the forest caused my heart to pound in my chest as a thought dawned on me, one I didn't want to believe, but knew must be true. Five minutes out, I received another phone call from the nurse on duty. My mother died overnight. Cause of death?

Exsanguination.

The message played on repeat, and I listened to every word she said each time. I picked up on the confusion in her voice, her inability to understand why the dreams seemed so real. This revelation helped me more than her, as it allowed me to be privy to knowledge hidden from me.

I'm the girl in the forest.

In another life, this woman, my mother, aborted me. My first drop didn't come on a cold winter evening. It came from her womb when they sucked me out of her. And she dropped, too, after dying on a table. Why? Because my mother made the mistake of existing in an era when a person's reproductive rights were in prohibition.

We laid Mom to rest next to my father. I waited a few weeks after the funeral, giving myself some time to mourn, before I continued with my quest. In hindsight I shouldn't have. In fact, I should have started from the top of my list and moved down. If I went by the numbers, I might have saved them all.

Verifying my high-school sweetheart's 'new' name only took a visit to our yearbook. Finding him proved to be far more difficult. He moved out of town a decade ago, after we broke up. A trip there led me to another state and back home, again, empty handed. I did learn horrible things. Of how he slipped into drug and alcohol abuse after our breakup. His family, who already thought of me as a harlot who cheated on their son, blamed me.

They weren't wrong about placing blame.

A light comes on in the shanty as the twilight of dusk casts gray shadows across the wooded lot. Smoke rises from a chimney, and the aroma of fresh burned timber mingles with the rotten stench permeating the air. Once the sun sets and the moon rises, I'll move closer, observe, and knock on the door. Hopefully he will not react in some maniacal manner. Until then, I continue to recollect my path to this juncture.

The trucker? Finding him promised to be nearly impossible. Without an identity or so much as a face, the only clue in my possession proved to be my memory of the regional company he drove for. Hoping it didn't change in my drops since, I sought them out, and as luck would have it, the place's name remained constant.

I returned to the scene of the drop. Truckers are creatures of habit, and once they find a road less traveled, they tend to continue taking it. This knowledge resulted in a new hobby I excelled at for a month: stalking. It started with me, sitting in a parking lot adjacent to the intersection at night, watching the trucks go by.

After the same truck from the same company barreled on through at roughly the same time on four consecutive nights, I felt confident I found him. The fifth night, I followed the truck.

It drove to the hub. I waited across the street in a used car dealer's stock lot, observing until the driver left in his minivan. At this time, I wouldn't follow him in his car. Not yet. After a week of learning his patterns, I noted a bumper sticker on the van.

THE DINER

The place turned out to be regional, declaring itself the 'home of the ten-cent coffee.' I moved my surveillance to their parking lot for a week, shifting around the hours blue collar workers typically change shifts.

And won't you know who showed up every day at three o'clock? My trucker. Today I sat inside, to get a good glimpse of him.

He arrived on time, and when I saw him, I knew it to be him. It brought my memory of the night back to life, because Finally I could put a face with the man from one of my lingering memories of dropping almost a decade ago.

Approaching the cabin might be a mistake, but I do it regardless. As I get closer, the nauseating stench kicks up a notch. I cover my nose and mouth with a wad of napkins from inside my purse. It's a poor filter, but better than nothing.

Stepping up onto the porch, I knock on the door. No one replies. A faint muttering, like someone is crying and sniffling, emanates from somewhere nearby, but I can't quite place where it might come from. I knock again, then step back and turn around.

And walk face first into him.

"This is whatchu get for thinking you was so smart snooping around. What you didn't know is I was looking for you, too. Too fuckin' easy!" He says, then swings a wooden baseball bat at my head. I see stars from the impact, and it knocks me the fuck out.

I wake and find myself chained to a radiator in what passes for a living room in the shanty. It reeks of piss, shit, and something else wretched I can't identify. Newspapers cover the floor in lieu of carpeting. Cobwebs decorate the walls, covering a respectable collection of old velvet portraits.

A thick patina of dust coats most of the paintings. The furniture in the place amounts to a piss-stained sofa sectional, complete with a listing coffee table covered in fast food bags and take out containers. A dining table stands to my left. And to my right, he sits in a wobbly rocking chair, watching me.

"**W**here am I?" I asked him.

"My family's camp on the lake. There ain't a soul within two, three miles of us. It's the only place I had left to go, after, well, after she left me," he said, and sniffled. He didn't exaggerate his assertion on the camp's isolation. When driving down the road earlier, I noticed the place took secluded to a new extreme.

"What's going on here?"

"Look at you, asking all these questions. Isn't it obvious? I've abducted you."

"Yeah, about that," I yanked on the chain attached to my wrist with a handcuff.

"You won't break it. Try all you want. Besides, you was stalking me. Or do you forget? For weeks. I saw your car too many times. I caught on. And I figured it would end up being you. You know something? Ten years ago, my life changed. I lost everything I ever had. All of it. I became a drunk and pissed it all away. Why? Because of you two sons of bitches. It's all I could do, numbing myself, trying to put myself back together."

"What are you talking about? I don't know who you are," I lied.

"You know damn well who I am and what I'm talking about missy. You know what you Goddamn did to me, too. I can't even kill myself without waking up like it's some sort of Groundhog Day bullshit, except the world kept moving on and the day didn't start over. And every fucking time it happens, you leave a little bit of yourself behind. So, I stopped killing myself, and Lord, that was fucking hard to do. But I did, I stopped it, and I started drinking, numbing my mind to it all. And you know what I found out?"

"The drinking doesn't stop the nightmares," I told him, speaking from personal experience.

"You bet your ass it doesn't stop the nightmares. But I found something that has. And now that I've got you, I think I can celebrate, just a little."

"And why is that?" I asked, "and why does it smell like a festering dumpster in here?"

"Ain't you a cute one. You know what? I stopped drinking the day I locked him in the shed. It's been a blessing."

"Wait a second, man," I said, "locked who in the shed? What are you talking about?" I tugged at the chain securing me to the radiator.

"I found a way. I stopped the cycle and the nightmares. For now," he said, ignoring my protests, "but there ain't too much of him left. Makes me glad I finally found you. I think after this is all said and done, I might be able to talk my wife into letting me go home. Maybe starting over. Do you think she'd take me back?"

"Let me out of here, you crazy fuck!" I demanded. He ignored the order, stood up from his chair and gathered some things around the sink. A bowl, some utensils. I think I saw a small carving knife, nothing to indicate he may want to murder me.

Wouldn't that be a son of a bitch, for this lunatic to send me on another drop. Karma has a way of catching up with you when you drop.

"Don't worry, I ain't gonna kill you. Can't have you spilling bad luck on me. No, no, no. I've learned something, if you simply expire, you know, die of natural causes, say from some prolonged disease or condition, maybe an ailment of some sort, do you know what happens?"

"It stops?"

"Yes. It stops," he sighed after announcing his theory. I assumed as much, myself, when pondering the nature of this awareness I believed to be unique to my psyche.

"Where are you going?" I asked, still tugging on the chain.

"I've got a regularly scheduled appointment with our mutual friend. You'll get a visitation soon, don't worry. If I'm going to be honest, I don't think he'll be too happy I lured you here. I feel for him, you know. He sort of blames you for all of this, too. But, then again, after what I've done to him," he shrugged his shoulders, "he's never all that happy to see anyone."

"Who are you talking about?"

"Just wait and you'll see," he cackled, and stepped out of a screen door on the back of the shanty. The rusty wires squealed, and the wood slapped against the frame as he let it slam shut behind him.

The shrill, petrified howling I hear can't possibly come from a human. But what else would it be? The being making the noise must be suffering in unimaginable ways.

I remember Houdini's trick to escaping handcuffs, he'd dislocate his thumbs. This method is easier to postulate than to apply. There's also picking the lock on the cuff. I scour the newspapers covering the floor until I find what I'm looking for.

Staples.

I retrieve a pair of them from the paper and unfold the metal. They're old, with a trace of rust and only a little fragile, but they'll work. I use one to displace the tumblers, and the other to release the lock.

It works. The cuff opens and I am free. My joy is short-lived. I hear him returning. Instead of a frontal confrontation, I prefer the element of surprise working in my favor. I close the cuff, sliding it over the wristlet, providing the illusion I am still chained up.

The screams continue as the screen door opens and the man returns with the bowl. I see a splash of blood along the side of it. He sets it down on the counter by the sink and washes his hands.

"What's in the bowl?" I asked him. I thought he'd ignore me. He didn't.

"You'll find out in due time," he said, "no need to worry about that now. You have other things to worry about. This is your new home, so get comfy in your corner while you still can."

"What do you mean, other things to worry about?"

"What are you, a child?" He turned from the sink, a carving knife in hand, "You're always asking questions, like a child. Well, I've got an answer for you, missy," he stepped toward me with the knife raised, "how do you like this?" He dropped his arm down and stabbed the wall next to my head.

"I've had about enough of your bullshit!" I said and swung at him with the hook of the handcuffs. The stainless-steel point punctured his eye. Pink liquid squirted out, prompting him to scream. He dropped the knife and bent over.

I kicked him in the face, sending him tumbling across the table and onto the floor. He stood up and charged at me, again. This time I caught him with the chain, delivering a solid blow to his head with the metal links. A handful of teeth spewed out of his mouth, leaving behind contrails of blood. The trucker fell to the newspapered floor. I cuffed both of his wrists, with his arms behind his back.

All of our car keys sat on a small end table next to his chair. I took them, and saw myself to the nearest exit, the rusty screen door.

"You ain't gonna like what you find out there, missy," the man cackled, "at least what's left."

"Do I look like I give any fucks? If you're lucky, you'll gnaw your arm off before the cops get here," I replied. He snickered, I gave him the finger and pushed the screen door open

"You won't be calling no police, missy."

The lingering stench grew stronger once I opened the door. A small, cluttered patio deck, if you could call it that, greeted me outside. On the other side of the deck stood a small, listing shed, one of the pre-built ones you find in a Home Depot parking lot. The origin of the stink, and all the trucker's secrets, loomed before me, hidden from view by the shed's doors.

—

What could be worse than dying and living over and over again? I think I found it today, inside the shed behind the shanty. Looking at him, chained to the wall of the shed, I can do nothing but throw a hand to my mouth and gasp.

Before me I see a wretched thing, gnarled and frail from captivity, sans his extremities. Gangrenous bandages, dripping with pus and infection, cover the stumps. Scars marking where chunks of meat were removed from muscles cover his chest. Separate tubes connect to his face and groin. One drips water into his mouth, the other allows the passage of waste. It doesn't go far, the latter empties into an overflowing cesspool in the floor.

He opens his eyes. I recognize him, my high-school sweetheart. Those eyes remained the same, though his name changed. Tears stream down my cheeks. I run to him, braving my repulsion of the conditions. He comes to life, rattling his chains, shaking his head, and howling. It's the same mournful wailing I heard before.

"I've got to get you out of here!" I screamed, crying.

"No!" he protests, each word followed by gasps for air. His lips are puffy and infected, and his eyes droop. "Don't! Don't touch me! Go away! Don't kill me! Please don't, please don't kill me!" I stopped in place, shocked at his reaction.

"What do you mean? I'm not going to kill you! Look at what he's done to you!"

"Don't you understand?" My old boyfriend pleaded to me, "if you kill me, I'll come back like this! I can't come back like this. If I just die, if you just leave me here and let me die, then it will all be over." I could see each word causing him more pain, as he breathed in more air to speak.

"How can you ask that of me? Doctors, they can save you." I understood now, but my instinct told me to parlay for his life.

"And what-" he choked on a bit of phlegm and coughed, "what kind of life would I have?"

"I can't believe he's been eating you." A roar of laughter I didn't think possible bellowed from him.

"Eating me? Is that what you thought?" He coughed as he laughed, "he hasn't been eating me. For the last year he's been feeding me to myself. He thinks it stops his nightmares. He says he's putting my pieces back together for me. All it does is bring my nightmares to life. Every fucking day at this time. And as you can plainly see, there's nothing left of me to carve off."

I don't say a word when I leave the shed and return to the shanty. He's crouched on the floor, which I find too convenient. Taking advantage of the moment, I kick the trucker in the face. It knocks him out. I don't want to kill him, not yet.

I drag him to the shed and chain him next to my ex.

"What will you do to him?" My ex asks. I say nothing. Instead, I walk away and inspect the tools stored in the shed. Hanging on the walls are the trucker's instruments of dismemberment. Bone saws and hacksaws, a giant cleaver, an assortment of knives and skewers. I reach up a finger and tick the blade of one. My ex cackles, agreeing with my decision.

I choose the cleaver first.

—

When I promised to stop killing myself, I couldn't have foreseen the impact such a choice would make. And yeah, things have been going great for me as a result. Now, I can't say the same for a certain individual at this moment in time, but me? I've been doing fine.

Sitting on a stool at the Diner, I'm taken by the aroma of ten cent coffee filling the air. My reflection in the mirror behind the counter has a few more white and gray hairs, and I'm okay with it. Anyone who has experienced what I have in the last few weeks would appreciate my composure. I look happier than in days before, of this much I'm certain.

"You've been coming here quite a bit lately," the waitress says, "that stool might as well have your name on it."

"You could say that," I reply.

"The usual?" She asks. I nod. She fills my glass with cold ice water. "I'll be back with your cherry pie soon as Cookie gets it out of the oven. Piping hot and fresh."

"Thank you," I say, and she walks away. I don't tell her this is the last day she'll see me.

My ex died in his sleep the night before. I hope he's free from this curse and didn't drop into another dismembered body. I found him when I came to feed the trucker a little bit more of himself this morning. I think the trucker's enjoying the calf stew. He doesn't know the menu is changing to bar-b-que today.

Three gallons of gasoline are now sitting in my trunk. There's enough to engulf the shanty and shed in a purifying blaze and incinerate everything there.

The trucker's not dead, yet. He's going to die today,

of that I'm certain. Once I eat my pie, I'll head back to the shanty for the last time and prepare the trucker for a one-way trip to his own personal Hell.

Over the last two weeks I've relieved him of his arms and legs and fed most of it to him. I want to be sure he'll suffer for what he did. If our theory is correct, he'll be reliving his dismembered immolation for eternity. It won't matter if his name changes, or his eyes turn color, or his sex changes or if the actor they get to play him in the made for TV movie is different. All he'll know is the pain and damnation of fire as he burns forever through infinite realities. And what if karma catches up with me for this?

I'll gladly pay the bill.

SOBRIQUET A LA MODE

Accompanied by a pair of men in suits, a middle-aged woman in a frumpy sun dress stepped into a room, her eyes agape. She stared forward, a tear forming in her eye.

"Good Lord," the woman gasped and froze in place.

"Mrs. Buffett?" the man in the suit asked.

She didn't move.

"What is it? Do you see something?"

"Ma'am? Is everything okay?" the other man asked her. "I know the situation here, it's an active crime scene, I know it might be—"

Elaine broke out of her trance. "Yes, I'm aware of what *this* is. I'm fine," she replied, interrupting the man. "I've seen worse."

"I don't know where you could've."

"Sugar, you have no idea what I've seen or heard."

"Alrighty then. This isn't how we normally carry out an investigation, but the family requested you be here.

Please don't disturb anything. We've got to, well, you know. Talk to her. Let us know if you see or hear anything or need something."

The woman nodded.

The men in suits stepped aside, then left the woman in the room, but she wasn't alone.

"Hey, ain't you that lady on that TV show, The Parahunters?" the man sitting at the table said.

"I am. Pleased to meet you. As you know, I'm Elaine. And you are?"

"Talking to you."

"Yes, you are."

"So, does this mean I'm gonna be on TV?"

"Well, I can't promise that, sugar. I don't make the final decisions. Our producer does."

"Oh, I didn't know that."

"It's okay, sugar. Now you do." Elaine winked at him and grinned.

"Sit down, ma'am, please. By all means, join us, why don'tcha?" the man continued. "We're—well *I'm*—supposed to do the talking now, right? That's the thing, isn't it? Me and all y'all in this room, and of course I'll start first because they ain't going to. So, we'll go with just me running my mouth from this point on until I finally admit I'm full of shit and we all say, *'There's no such thing as no ghosts,'* or so *they* say. Folks say sometimes you can't see the things right in front of yer face, but the same notion applies to hearing things. And none of y'all ever get it. Shit, all I can hear is crying babies, and I've had to ignore that, so I can't blame ya."

"I can hear it, too, the crying."

"You can?"

"I can," the woman added, nodding. "Do you mind if I take notes? I don't want to forget anything you tell me."

"No, not at all. Take all the notes you want. It's funny, ya know, I know I saw what I saw, that I lived what I lived—and my experience tells me fucking ghosts do exist—but *they*, the motherfucking critical thinkers, the naysayers, they don't give two shits. No matter what evidence you provide to the contrary, *they* always double down like a horse with blinders. And why? *Cos there ain't no such thing as no ghosts.* Right?"

"Not everyone is as open minded as some of us."

"That's right! Who the fuck are *they*, anyways? I gotta say this, I'm none too partial to the selective omniscience bequeathed upon *them*. *They* can't accept that possibility, because *they* won't subscribe to the theory that life continues after death. But it does, and I know it does, and if me and Birdie here had been left be, none of y'all'd be in this fuckin' room with us, now would ya? I didn't think so. You wouldn't be sitting there watching the hours tick away, waiting for *me* to incriminate myself when none of ya will hear a damn word I say anyways. *'Anything you say will be used against you in a court of law,'* right?"

"Well, it is the law; they're required to read that to a person so they know their rights," Elaine answered. "But, I'm not a police officer."

"No, yer not. But I know why they sent you here. I've watched enough TV. So, if that's what *they* want ya to get outta me, then let me indulge all you. I wouldn't want to waste yer precious time, right? And since none of *ya* ever want to believe the truth, I'll pretend I'm lying so ya listen to what I've got to say. In the meantime, you pretend I'm not lying and I'll pretend y'all give a shit. Jesus, I'm rambling, ain't I?"

"Just a little, but that's okay. I didn't catch your name."

"I didn't give it to you."

"No, you didn't."

"So, I guess we'll get to the point, hah?"

"That works for me, sugar." Elaine brought the pen to the paper of the notebook on the table.

"Where do I begin? Where does this shit show start? When I met Birdie? Is that where? Or later on with the real juicy parts? Truth be told, what we did started back then, when we first saw each other on the city bus, so that's the best spot, I think."

"Excellent, a great starting point."

"Damn, she was—well she *is*—beautiful! Just look at her, why don'tcha." He pointed to Birdie, sitting in the parlor, talking to the men in suits.

Elaine acknowledged and nodded. "How about you just tell me everything that happened, I won't say a word from here on out. And we let them worry about Birdie. You talk to me; they'll talk to her. Deal?"

"Deal."

"**I** saw Birdie on my way to work about a week before the pandemic hit. She was with her friend and the girls were watching me watch them touch each other in places proper ladies shouldn't be exposing in public.

'*Hi, I'm Birdie,*' she said.

She does talk, believe you me, even though she ain't talking to y'all right now.

'*I'm-*' she shook her head and placed the finger she'd been diddling herself with on my lips. She tasted so sweet. '*Ya like that?*' she asked.

I nodded because I did.

She asked if I'd like to see more of it at their place and I said I would. So, I no-showed my job and later learned I got fired. I didn't care. Everyone got unemployment during the pandemic.

Two hours later, she watched me fuck her friend. I can't remember the girl's name. At first, I kinda put that out of my head, especially when we, well, when we did what we did later. But come to think of it, I never got her name, not once.

Liking what she saw, Birdie sat on her face, grinding down on the girl while I pounded on her fat cunt. She was thrashing in ecstasy and I felt her clench up on me, squirting all over my cock. So, I popped my nut and didn't think nothing of it. Well, not until later when the three of us was cuddling.

Something stunk like dog shit, waking me up. I noticed Birdie's friend got ice cold and stiff between then and when we finished. Women ain't supposed to get stiff after fucking, or cold.

When she didn't get up and I found runny shit between her legs, I kinda panicked, not sure what we should do about a dead body. Her face was blue, so it was obvious we killed her while fucking. We both saw what happened to people who couldn't afford lawyers. They'd get a goddamn public defender who ends up getting them the death penalty. We were freaking out pretty hardcore. Then, Birdie came up with the idea, and now that I think of it, I'm pretty sure that wasn't the first time she'd done it.

We couldn't report the incident, they'd blame us, of course, and we'd go to jail. We had to do something about her body. So, we did.

Now, let me make this clear, before ya go on thinking this was my fucking idea. It wasn't, and something tells me this was Birdie's plan all along. I know I didn't go into this thinking, *'Oh, I want to literally eat people,'* or nothing like that. But desperate people do desperate things and, with the pandemic going on, well, ya know.

In the garage, Birdie's grampa had a whole bunch of saws and shit. We sliced and chopped up the dead fuck toy and put her parts in the chest freezer. There was surprisingly little blood; by then, it had thickened in her veins and turned to a black goo. It spit around the room, flinging off the saw blade. The process covered us in little black dots that smelled like burned liver. But damn, they were delicious little morsels, tasting sweet and coppery.

So, we chopped her up and packaged the cuts, froze the meat, and stored it in the chest freezer. And through the first part of the pandemic, we didn't need to get no meat from the store cos a hundred-and-eighty-pound woman goes pretty far for two people. We wasted nothing. Shit, we even turned her bones into our own personal jelly recipe.

This was what, three years ago, now? She fed us for months. I mean she was fuckin' delicious. They say human tastes like pork, right? And pork tastes like what ya dress it in, so she tasted like spiced rub, or a Bit O' Honey, which did wonders turning her shoulder into a ham. So, we fucked and ate like a king and queen.

Well, we did until we ran out of meat.

Since we ate the last of her, meat from the grocery store just didn't taste right anymore. Beef had a processed flavor and pork tasted spoiled. Chicken was so bland nothing could make it taste like anything but rubber. And after a year of eating fresh, untainted meat, we were growing hungry for more.

We made do with what we could get for delivery. We didn't need to worry about money for basics, what with us both getting unemployment. When the delivery guy came with our groceries was when Birdie and me both saw it. The ghost of her friend pointing at him, then she stood in front of him, shaking her head as if to say, *'No!'* I couldn't believe my eyes. A fucking gho—"

"**W**ait, you saw and heard the ghost then?" Elaine interrupted the interview, her eyes wide with curiosity.

"No, no, Mrs. Buffett. We saw them, but we didn't hear them."

"You both saw them? That's remarkable. Spirits don't often reveal themselves in such a manner."

"Yep," he agreed, "I've learned a ton about ghosts since then."

"You have? Indulge me some, why don't you."

"So, ya can't hear them cos even though they can talk, and think ya can hear them, they aren't breathing, and sound is made by air vibrating, right? So, all it looks like is they're running their mouth, and nothing is coming out."

"Okay, that's right," she sighed in relief. In her experiences with spirits in the afterlife, she knew certain things were a constant when dealing with the paranormal. The most important being ghosts couldn't be heard in our world. But in that world in-between, the one Elaine strode, you could hear them clear as day.

"This doesn't mean they can't communicate."

"Right, or else we—" Elaine started to say, then stopped.

"Or else we what?"

"Oh, never mind, it's nothing we can't address later. What else happened?"

"Well, as the ghost pointed out to us, the grocery delivery guy was off limits with a shake of her see-through head. If we took him down and dressed him, he'd, for sure, be looked for with his final destination being our place."

"That's so true. You've got to cover your tracks, right?"

"Right," he nodded in agreement.

"What did you do next?"

"The whore we found on the cruising site, he was a different story."

Elaine listened and wrote.

"We used a burner account and a VPN to cover our tracks. We picked him up in record time. When he showed up at our place, the friend's ghost was elated, waiting for someone to join her, trapped in this house on the other side. You know how that works, don't you? How ghosts get trapped in the places they died? Of course you do, I'm sorry, I'm getting off topic.

Any hoot, he took our cash and we all got naked, even the ghost. We fucked him for hours, and when the time was right, we wanted to try out a theory.

I'd always heard a person has an orgasm as they die. I kinda experienced it that first day together with Birdie, but we didn't know the result at the time. So, this time we planned it. We asked the whore to fuck me, and he obliged. Birdie came up behind him and sliced his throat when he was banging my ass. I felt him clench up as he died, and sure as shit, he arched his back and thrust into my prostate, making me come in unison. The dead man came a bucket as the blood drained from his body. Birdie licked it all out of my crack after his corpse slipped out of me.

We ate some of him raw on the spot. God, it tasted so fucking good, raw and fresh. The blood dripped down my chin after I bit off his testicles. Birdie and I shared his balls.

Then we cleaned his phone and hid his car at a local gay cruising spot, and no one was the wiser.

Later, after chopping him up and storing nearly two hundred pounds of meat, we experimented. Birdie found super gourmet recipes on TikTok or Pinterest and we tried them all. The pork and chicken recipes were always the best.

A few months later, we noticed the ghost of Birdie's friend could be found lying with its head against Birdie's belly. It was then that Birdie told me about the pregnancy. I was elated. We were going to have a little one of us running around! Birdie lactated a lot, and I couldn't let that go to waste. So, I nursed on her whenever we'd fuck. She loved it and so did I.

The whore's ghost appeared soon after we ate the last of him. He'd show up with Birdie's dead friend, rubbing Birdie's baby bump, their tongues lolling out of their ghost mouths, like they both knew something we didn't.

When the time came and her water broke, we were prepared. Birdie pushed the baby out. I never realized how much blood and slimy fluid came out of a woman giving birth. I slapped its ass and it cried. Before handing the baby over to his mother, I cleaned off the placenta and cut the umbilical cord. Later we put them in a soup. It was the best soup either of us ever ate, even better than any of the cuts of meat from the whore or Birdie's friend.

That night, when the baby wouldn't stop crying, Birdie came up with a solution to the crying:

Bake it.

Of course, the ghosts influenced her decision, they pointed to the baby then to the roasting pan, encouraging us to do the unthinkable. But we were out of good meat and knew a nine-pound roast would feed us for at least a week. So, we wrapped it up in a bed of veggies when it finally fell asleep. It woke screaming when we closed the preheated oven's door. The crying was replaced by an aromatic sizzle about fifteen minutes later.

God-fucking-damn did it taste good. I can't remember the baby's sex, but I can remember how succulent and tender its flesh was. I do remember we fucked hard after, even though Birdie's cunt was a torn-up mess from giving birth to that week's dinner. I came twice on one hard-on; the semen mixed with her blood and created a soup that smelled like sex and copper.

We saw the baby's ghost in the arms of Birdie's dead friend soon after we gobbled down the last of it. They looked like a happy ghost family, the whore and Birdie's friend and their new baby. At least we couldn't hear the baby crying anymore, that was a good thing. All was well, but after a couple days passed, we learned the ghosts could hear the baby's non-stop screeching on the other side and it was driving them up the fucking walls.

Our once benign spirits got all violent and shit, throwing shit off the walls, smashing doors and slamming windows. The ghosts wanted more from us, something to make the baby happy. And to make things worse, the ghostly baby kept reaching out for Birdie or for me. It was obvious what needed to be done.

Over the following days, while we were fucking, we could see the ghosts taunting us, wanting what only we could give them. So, we fucked until she got a positive pregnancy test back. This quieted the ghosts down some, but it didn't solve our own problem. So, we looked for another slab of meat on the cruising site.

We found a couple looking to swing this time. Couples were different from single whores. Ya had to schmoose them a little before going in for the kill. So, the first couple times we got together as couples, we played in the same room while a trio of ghost voyeurs stood in the room saying things no one could hear but them.

Birdie caught me using the wife's name while we were on the phone.

'What did I tell ya about names, lover boy?' She asked. I shrugged my shoulders, not sure where she was going with this. *'Ya don't give yer food a name. Makes it harder for ya to put 'em down when the time comes. This was the first thing I learned growing up on the farm with the cows and chickens.'*

This made sense to me then and makes a whole helluva lot more sense to me now, sitting here telling ya about it all. But I'm getting ahead of myself now, ain't I? I took her advice and used a pet name for the wife going forward. She didn't seem to mind it.

After establishing the relationships, Birdie and I decided we'd tag them separately, using a ruse to get them over to the house without the other. After all, taking down one person was easier than two. The plan was to lure them over and take them out one at a time. So, I spent a week telling the wife how much I wanted to leave Birdie, and Birdie spent a week telling the husband how much she wanted to leave me for him. It was fool proof.

But, the ghosts had other plans.

The husband was plowing Birdie's field with his fuck stick, bringing her to the brink of orgasm when I came up behind him and stabbed him in the back of the neck, severing his spinal column from his brain stem. Blood sprayed all over the walls as he thrashed about from each surprise blow. His body spasmed and came, filling Birdie's eager cunt with his jizz. When he finally stopped moving, I tossed his dead body aside and snowballed his spunk out of her, spitting it back in her mouth before kissing her deeply.

We didn't have the time to chop his body up before luring his wife in, so we stored him whole in the chest freezer, figuring we'd slice them up together. We could have three good years of meat out of these two, for sure, and with another baby on the way, we'd have a nice holiday roast, too.

This is where we learned the ghosts didn't want the wife around, and they did everything they could to ruin the moment. The poltergeist bullshit started soon after she arrived. Paintings flying off the wall tend to put the fear of the unknown into people when they aren't expecting it.

Once we got naked, and she was done sucking my cock dry, it was evident she was getting cold feet over leaving her husband. I've wondered if she would have reacted differently if she'd known he was already dead and waiting for her to join him. As we continued to fuck, I was getting nervous myself, well more anxious, wanting to take her out so we could get on with cutting their bodies up. But then, after sex during our pillow talk, she spilled the beans and told me what was bothering her. She was pregnant and not sure if it was mine or her husband's.

This elated me. I think my immediate smile and enthusiasm scared her. After all, she was concerned over the baby's parentage. I, on the other hand, was salivating… thinking of another tender cooked roast.

Putting her clothes back on, she fully intended on leaving our place, when Birdie's presence surprised her. Birdie smacked the wife in the head with a cast iron frying pan, knocking her out cold. The blow crushed her jaw and knocked out most of her teeth. The act brought my cock back to life.

I took advantage of the moment and fucked the unconscious woman's mangled mouth. It was wet and each thrust sent bloody snot out of her nose. I could feel her teeth scraping along the length of my cock as I got off. She made sounds like a snuffling pug as my ejaculation came out her nose with blood covered teeth.

Birdie fucked the handle of the frying pan while she watched me get off.

We tied the wife up and decided not to kill her, not yet. She did get a front row seat to the dismemberment and dressing of her husband. We even fed her his testicles, pureeing them with a blender with a shit ton of antibiotics to kill any infections. She didn't argue with us once and did as she was told. Even though she knew what she was sucking down a straw, the smoothie was pretty tasty.

I was proud of her for not crying while we did it, and for drinking the whole smoothie. Well, she couldn't do much of anything with her mouth being all fucked up like it was, with her blood and my cum dripping out of her nose and down her chin.

I took care of their cars, driving them to separate whore-tels a couple counties away. When I was gone, Birdie made sure our new house guest was comfortable and would be for the next eight or so months. Birdie would give birth a few weeks before our guest, and we were aiming to have a great holiday feast come the end of the year.

We had rules for our guest. She'd be kept alive; we could feed her Pedialyte with a tube shoved down her throat. We kept our promise, and she wasn't abused in any manner. We didn't want to risk losing her gift to us, so no sex, nothing to stress her out more than she already was being held captive in a cannibal's basement.

As the months passed, her jaw healed, and she could chew with half her mouth again. At first, our guest wouldn't take the meat we fed her, but after she lost a considerable amount of weight and grew desperate, she finally gave in. I imagine its taste was as cathartic for her as it was for Birdie and me. She ate it willingly from here on, regardless of its origin.

As she neared term, we realized feeding three mouths taxed our meat supply. We took her legs while she slept one night. Her husband's ghost watched as we did it, his face a grimace of agony.

Normally we don't get fresh, unfrozen meat, and it

was delicious. She even ate it, not realizing her own legs made the main course. Covered up with a blanket, she couldn't see what we had done to her legs. The phantom sensations tricked her into thinking we had only broken them to prevent her from escaping. I wasn't about to tell her otherwise.

Then, it happened. Birdie went into labor a few weeks early. Everything about this pregnancy was different from the first one. We found out why when she passed a stillborn baby. At first, Birdie was upset. Then she realized all we needed to do was toss it in the roasting pan. But the end result wasn't as our family of ghosts wanted.

This is where I learned stillborns don't make ghosts. The spiritual baby, longing for companionship, was denied, at least for the time being. The end product was a little tougher than I would've liked when it came out of the oven. We chalked it up to being a fetal thing.

A month later, when the wife gave birth, she didn't care about her legs so much as she cared about holding her baby. We let her and watched as the baby's ghostly father's hands passed through his child's body. She didn't want to give the baby up, holding it close to her face as I tried to take it back. Birdie gave me a knife, and then, as I cut the umbilical cord, I sliced the mother's throat. We bled her out on the spot, and while I prepped the baby for the roasting pan, Birdie chopped the rest of the wife up and placed her in the freezer.

Goddamn was that roast as good as the first one, not tough at all. We ate it and fucked on the table after. Yeah, we had this down to a science now. The baby's mother lasted us until a few weeks ago. Now, a pair of ghost babies cuddled together, sucking on a ghost teat from the mother of one of them. All was well in the house.

When her ghost showed up, we knew it was time to lure someone else into our fold and fill the freezer. With the pandemic ending, it was getting harder to find easy targets.

My unemployment ran out and we were starting to get into money troubles. Feeding two mouths was easier when we had at least some money coming in. Now, it was nearly impossible to do.

Birdie and I did what we could do to get by; that included eating as little possible and fucking as often as we could, which meant all day long in the grand scheme of things. We'd fuck, then we'd rest, and fuck again.

I can remember the last time we fucked like it was yesterday. Birdie sat on top, cowgirl, riding me and ramming my cock into her dirt hole. She spread her pussy wide for me to look at it gape and pulse while she came, her ass skewered on my throbbing pole. She squirted all over me in fountains gushing from her cunt.

I was too busy paying attention to my cock getting ready to come when something hit me in the side of the head. The orgasm that followed was better than any I'd ever experienced. I closed my eyes and felt it tear through every nerve in my body, and something occurred to me, as I faded from one world into another. A final epiphany grew in my being, and I knew what she planned all along…

Birdie never knew my name. In three years, she never once spoke it. She called me all sorts of names. Honey, baby, lover… but never by my name. All pet names. Nicknames."

Elaine turned the page and continued jotting down the story as it was told to her. She looked up to see the others standing behind him, wishing none of what he told her was true, but their presence proved him to be honest.

"Time changed from then and now to forever. I woke up today and now we're here, in this room, and I'm still talking and nobody's listening, are they?"

"I'm listening to you, Mike."

"How do you know my name? I haven't heard it in so long."

"There's lots I know. You must understand why I'm here? They," she gestured to the spirits standing behind him, "certainly do. The detectives talking to Birdie—"

"What about them?" he cut in. "It's because none of them can hear a goddamn word I'm saying. Right? Well, some of ya can. The ghosts of four other adults and a pair of newborns, they can hear everything I say. I'm the preacher and they're my righteous choir, like that does any of us any fucking good."

"Hallelujah, Pastor Mike!" Elaine chuckled. "I'm playing the organ. You said it yourself, they wouldn't believe you if you told them. Shit, they wouldn't even be able to hear you. But you told me, didn't you? And I could hear you because that's what I can do. That's why I have a TV show, right?"

"That's right, Mrs. Buffett," Mike admitted. "That's right."

"Exactly. And I wrote it all down here, didn't I?" She pointed to the notebook.

"Yes, you did. They didn't even want ya here, did they." Mike's words were more of a statement than a question.

"That's right. Your family actually requested I come. They tracked your unemployment checks to this address and the cops are using that for the time being as probable cause to be here and talk to Birdie. But yes, to keep their true purpose a secret, they brought me along to placate your folks."

"I miss them. I wish I could see them again."

"You will, some day."

A nervous giggle slipped out of Mike's ethereal lips, "Ya know what I *can* see? I can see Birdie sitting at the kitchen table with all y'all's buddies listening to her lie, denying any of this ever happened, asking for an attorney. And ya know what kills me? If any of y'all believed in ghosts, if y'all weren't tainted by what *they* tell ya, y'all'd know everything I told ya is true."

"I believe in ghosts, Mike, you know I do. We wouldn't be talking if I didn't."

"And then there she is with her smug little face. Birdie, sitting there with yer mouth closed, waiting for yer lawyer to arrive. Even with a lawyer, something tells me they don't buy one bit of yer bullshit, Birdie, not one bit. They'll get a search warrant, I'm sure."

"One is on the way now," Elaine informed him.

"Ya know what, Mrs. Buffett?"

"What's that, Mike?"

"I bet if we, me and them," he pointed over his shoulder to the other spirits trapped in the walls of the house, "if we go down to the basement right now and move a couple things, the folks interviewing Birdie might want to go and investigate what *they* hear. I bet they won't need that search warrant to arrive, now will they. Come on, I'm sure ya heard about something called probable cause before. And who knows? After they find what they find, maybe *they'll* come around and say it was a ghost that led them to solving a few mysteries. Even though *they* don't believe in ghosts. Now, if y'all will excuse me, me and my friends have got a mess to make."

"I bet they will," Elaine assured him.

"We'll talk again, real soon, ma'am, I'm sure."

Elaine Buffett closed her notebook and watched as the ghost of Michael Bradley dissolved into the floor and disappeared. A half dozen other spirits followed before she could take her next breath. Moments later, a crashing din erupted from the basement. As predicted, it caught the attention of the detectives interrogating Birdie in the next room. They stood in unison and turned to the basement door.

"Sooner than later, sug—" she stopped the pet name in midbreath, and corrected herself. "Mike," Elaine said, sticking the pen behind her ear. She repeated herself as she stood, placing an emphasis on the first word, "*Sooner* than later, indeed."

WHAT FRAGILE BEINGS ARE WE

Life is good, I tell myself. I'm lying, of course. But all good lies are rooted in truth. I mean, the ingredients to a good life are present. The Rolling Stones are playing on the radio, an aural testament to this. It's something off Sticky Fingers, with tinny guitars and upbeat hooks. The sun is shining bright in the blue sky, and life is… good. I smile and assure myself this is the case. Yes, the day is pristine, with a comfortable, light breeze. And still, my mind wanders, and though the Stones fill my ears, another melody lingers in my mind. It's mesmerizing…

Their song. I can almost hear it. And I know somewhere, they're singing it, again. And thus my lie.

I'm certain if I listen closely I'll catch it, but I'll have to be resourceful. Solid mass moves sound better than air, or so I learned in tech school. I turn off the radio, climb out of my service van and put my ear to the green grass covering the ground. To see if their song is there. The grass is plush and caresses my cheek, the ground soft and welcoming.

And there it is… in the distance… ever so faint, but it is there…

…*Haunting me.*

Their melody resonates through the earth. It's beautiful and serene. It's not much different than say the wailing cries of whales in the deep oceans. It calls to me as it did the day I first heard it. It seems so long ago, the faithful day we became entwined.

Truth be told, it's been a week since I took the job. One week since I first stepped foot in the house on Danforth Circle. A week has seemed an eternity without them. Without their song. A distant yearning grows, nagging at me to follow it, to seek it out. I fully understand the misery of living without their song. It's an experience I no longer wish to endure…

I lay on the ground, listening, soaking it in like it's the morning sun filling me with Vitamin D. I drift off from this day to another, not so long ago. My memories circumvent space, and time, to replay the event in the traditional manner. I close my eyes and daydream to the subterranean melody calling out to me, further enabling the lie as I recall the events leading to today…

The call came in earlier in the day. I needed to check the exterior coaxial lines at a client's house on my way back from my last job. His internet shit the bed, and our inhouse tech discovered a problem with the line going in.

I would pass the address on my way home to Fulton from Fair Haven. This made it convenient for both myself and Mr. Michael Morrow, the impatient homeowner in Fenton, New York. Most DNS errors at residential locations ended up being user error or squirrel related, and thus quick fixes.

The afternoon install went long and I arrived at the Morrow home on Danforth Circle later than I planned. I drove the company van into a neighborhood I knew well. Its gentry reputation preceded it. And this cul de sac with a trio of homes, the Morrow property setting in the middle? Its fame meter and musical pedigree sat pretty high up there. I never heard of him before today, but he must've made a butt-load of dough doing what he did. The home to the left belonged to the estate of the former Papa John Phillips, and the home to the right to Steve Page, formerly of Bare Naked Ladies.

The Phillips home's reputation for domestic violence and juvenile pranking brought the police here often. Usually, you could attribute this to his actress daughter McKenzie and one of her washed-up rock-star boyfriends would drink too much and have a slobber knocker. If it wasn't a drunken domestic dispute in the Phillips house, the local kids egged or toilet papered the property. I can attest to this. I'm guilty of the latter.

This heightened police presence in the suburban community led to Page's own arrest for drugs and crude acts. Okay, let's call a spade a spade. Steve Page and his wife bought a hooker, a ton of blow, and brought them both back to their brand new home. Lost in the moment, they made the mistake of leaving the car running and the front door open. The patrolling cops walked in to see Mrs. Page sitting on the prostitute's face, her husband snorting lines off the naked whore's belly. Instead of a menage a trois, they spent the night in separate cells in the Onondaga County jail.

Having this knowledge, at the time, I could only imagine what decadence and debauchery hid behind the walls of the country estate owned by a man I would learn to call 'Mad' Mike Morrow. The Jeff Andrews whom I existed as a week ago stood unprepared for the terrifying experience to come within the labyrinthian tunnels of Morrow's cyclopean home. Of secrets and answers. The knowledge the Jeff Andrews I am today wishes he could forget…

I didn't have to knock on the door or ring the bell. Dressed in khaki shorts and a faded, blue tank top, Morrow stood on the stoop, arms crossed and lips pursed. A middle-aged, balding man, whose remaining hair matched the silver of his trimmed beard, Morrow beckoned me with frantic motions. Cold, steel blue eyes framed by shaggy grey brows blinked in sync with his palsy. His slippered feet scraped across the concrete of the stoop to complete the orchestra making up the Mike Morrow.

"Hurry, we've not much time! I need this remedy before nightfall, or I fear the worst will happen!" His words, coated in a tone of urgency, gave me a shiver and raised the small hairs on my neck and arms.

"Simmer down, sir, I can handle this," I brought up my

tablet and reviewed his complaint. A typical report played out before my eyes. DNS Errors. The strength of the internet signal to his basement, his upload and download speeds, and, of course, a buffering problem.

"You can fix all this within an hour? I find it highly unlikely you could, but it needs to be done, and the longer we stand here and talk the less time we have. Oh, my dear Margie," he said as a tear formed in his eye. He wiped it away with a gaunt hand, pocked with aging spots, "I never should have upgraded the locks. Stupid technology! Sometimes the old fashioned way is the best way."

"Let me see what I can do," I told him. I wasn't sure what his problem could be. I didn't want to know.

Now I can't forget it.

"Please, please, let me get out of your way."

"That's the best thing I've heard all day, let me get to work. I wish more clients were as considerate as you. I'll be starting outside," I declared. I returned to my van and grabbed my tool kit and a ladder. I already knew the answer to most of the problems Mr. Morrow experienced with his connection.

A bird's nest grew where the external line met the house. I leaned the ladder against the wall and climbed. I think this is the final point where I can say the job transformed from the mundane into anything other than normal.

Their song…

I heard a distant melody. It didn't come from anyplace in particular. It came from everywhere. I felt it through the ladder's aluminum rungs, in my fingers and palms. It pulsed with the melody, electrifying my shins and sending shocks through my boots, into my feet. The song moved through me, entering my flesh at the points of contact on the ladder.

I turned my head down, looking at the ground. A window on the side of the house below me caught my eye. I saw the flickering image of a woman through the window. She faded in and out with each of my breaths. Tall, with long yellow hair, and dressed in flowing white linens, she wept. Her song resonated through my being and in it I heard reflections of this woman's deep grief.

My Grandfather Andrews, fresh off the boat from Ireland, would see this, *hear this*, and declare her a Banshee. He would be right. He might've told me not to succumb to her Harpy's cry. Or not to look at the Banshee in her cold, dead eyes. Or to run away at first sight of the creature. Or given me countless other warnings in a similar tone.

My eyes found hers and I fell into a trance, staring at this apparition I shouldn't be seeing.

A rapping on the ladder broke me from my trance. I blinked, and she, too, disappeared.

"I don't understand how my problem can be outside when it's the basement that's having the trouble with the internet." Mr. Morrow said. I wanted to ignore him. Instead, I cleared the bird's nest out as he protested, "what are you doing?" The debris scattered on the ground, "Those birds are Margie's favorites! What do I say to her? Oh, Lord. What have you done!" and I discovered the chewed up coaxial line.

"It's because the birds severed part of your cable line." I showed him the black rubber picked away and the exposed wire. "This will only take me ten minutes to splice, then we'll check out the wifi inside."

"You mean the internet?" He questioned.

"Yes, that's what I mean." He really didn't know the difference between the two. I tried not to roll my eyes. I failed.

"Okay, I saw it. Now hurry, we haven't much time. The sun will be set soon and this needs to be finished!" Morrow chastised me, left, and disappeared into his house.

I finished the splicing in record time. Now I would need to check the router inside. Things started looking up for me. But it would take my hand turning the doorknob, and my feet stepping across the threshold of a mad man's home, for me to fully appreciate the insanity to come. It didn't waste a second in doing so after the door opened...

It assaulted my senses.

Ill-lit, the interior decorating of the house took cues from every imaginable hoarding cable tv series. Towers of aging, musty paper boxes lined the walls. A cat once roamed these halls, the lingering aroma of kitty piss watered my eyes.

Yet everywhere I went, I could feel the song, again. The melody, so familiar, yet fleeting. It filled the home, ebbing and flowing in strength, a constant ambient background noise. It's like seeing a bright star in your peripheral vision, and the fucking thing disappears when you look straight at it.

Using my flashlight to brave the way, I sought out the router and discovered it next to a writing desk in an old office. Within this room, a single wall stood devoid of boxes. Instead, a tall bookshelf, lined with books on fringe physics, quantum mechanics, and other sciences often scoffed at by more reputable sources.

Next to it, a cleared space on the wall caught my attention. A framed diploma from Arkham University, a Ph.D. in something Latin, hung next to a painting of a younger mister, excuse me-Dr. Morrow-embracing a tall, beautiful, blonde woman. The lady bore a strong resemblance to the ghostly figure I saw outside. The proverbial police line-up would have sealed this woman's fate as the culprit. Stunned, I stared at her in Dr. Morrow's arms for a few minutes, until I broke the silence.

"She's pretty," I said out loud, "lucky guy." Fumbling, I dropped my flashlight and discovered a stack of used desktop calendar pages sat on a nearby small table. Each day marked with a letter M, P, or D, with an 'X' marked through the squares. A fresh calendar half marked up and up to date adorned the desk's top. Pages of blueprints and schematics, wrinkled and aged, pushed aside in some previous chaotic event. Morrow's passport lay open on the desk. Stamps from ten years earlier for Argentina, Peru, and Mexico adorned the booklet's pages. The doctor got around.

"That's Margaret. My wife. And yes. She was pretty," Morrow piped in. He developed an odd habit of showing up at the right moment to startle me, "you don't need to pay no mind about those papers, please. Just take care of the router."

"Jesus, man. You scared the hell out of me." I jumped and hit my funny bone on a wayward box corner. I dropped the flashlight for a second time, a result of the stinger. It rolled across the floor. "I keep getting my ass kicked by an inanimate object with no moving parts." I picked it back up and slapped the black metal.

"Sorry," he stuttered his words. Fear shook them. But fear of what I didn't know, "just you never mind about them papers," for a genius, his choices in words lined up with a redneck, third-grade drop-out.

I never gave a shit about them until you made them a problem for me, I thought to myself and shook my head. The router stood behind the calendar pages. I pushed it aside with my shoulder.

"What did I just tell you? Never mind with-" I cut him off.

"I have to get to the router. This stack of paper is in the way. Now, if you would excuse me, I recall you wanted this done by dark? That's in less than an hour."

"Yes, yes," he stammered, "you are right, sir. Sorry, I'm so sorry." And again, Dr. Morrow shuffled away, disappearing to an undisclosed location within this hoarder's paradise. I rebooted the router, and as I waited for it to return to life, my mind wandered. I could feel, more than hear, the faint melody, distant and lonesome, through the floorboards.

A stack of worn photo albums sat next to the desk.

On top of the pile, a handful of polaroid prints lay. The woman, Mrs. Morrow herself, Margaret, at various stages of her life. A young woman walking dogs, a mother with babies in her arms, and a matron in the hospital. I felt my heart sink, and a tear formed in my eye.

M, P, and D floated about in my mind. The letters swirled around each other, orbiting and shifting position. They burned into the monitor within my brain, transforming into faded, gray clouds. What did they mean? They might be as innocuous as a record of meds he took. Or, perhaps, a record of sinister acts played out in this labyrinth of paper boxes.

I could only be certain of the obvious. For example, far more M's and P's than D's scrawled in the dates. Therefore, I could safely assume D designated a relatively new addition to the pattern. I wondered if these letters connected to the ghostly woman I may have hallucinated earlier. The first letter of Margie is 'M'. Could these be names on his calendar? Could each name correspond to a person? His collection of dead wives, maybe?

The router came to life, breaking me from my thoughts. It crackled and hissed, sounding like an angry cybernetic reptile. The unit's lights lit up in succession, from red to green. The noise stopped. I called for the home's owner. This time I wasn't surprised when he appeared out of nowhere, emerging from one of the many passageways within his domicile.

"Is it fixed?" He asked.

"Almost done." I answered, then my curiosity got the best of me, "what are you a doctor of?"

"Quantum Physics. I was an engineer for F-LAB, an American extension of CERN. Until other things became more," he paused, "important. And complicated. I left F-LAB and brought my work home."

"That's neat. A regular NASA type scientist."

"You could say that, yes."

"Can you make a spaceship?"

"In a sense, yes, I already have, before, for F-LAB."

"Really?" I couldn't believe how a man could invent a spaceship, but got his ass kicked by a router.

"Yes, really. The time, sir. We are pressed for it," Dr. Morrow tapped his analog watch.

"Yes. So listen, I need to go down to the basement and check the wifi signal strength and we'll be all set."

"You shouldn't go into the basement. It's a mess down there."

"Then I can't fix your internet?" I phrased it as a question, hoping he'd understand, "Isn't that where you are having connection problems?" A sincere question, "Then I need to check it. Can you show me how to get there?" Morrow hesitantly nodded in agreement, then huffed and begged me to follow him into the bowels of his home. I let him take the lead and trotted behind him.

The aroma of something other than musty papers tickled my nose. As we neared the kitchen, I realized Morrow exercised his culinary skills now more than his scientific. Something boiled, and I could smell cabbage and baking bread. Dinner time approached. We stopped before entering.

"Here we are," Morrow muttered.

"That smells delicious. What are you cooking?"

"Margaret's favorite. I cook for her every day."

"Oh? What's that?"

"Boiled brisket and cabbage, with potatoes and carrots. And a fresh-baked loaf of bread with butter."

"Margaret has good taste."

"Had. She's been dead a dozen or so years now," he turned his head down. After hearing his less than enthusiastic reply, I felt relieved I didn't slip earlier and ask where she may be.

Located outside the kitchen, the cellar's door presented itself as an entrance to Hell. I wondered where Dr. Morrow's three-headed dog might be hiding. The absence of a guardian hellhound did nothing to lessen the creepy level. Letters and numbers scrawled into the jam, written in black ink or carved into the wood. The words surrounded the basement door. A crucifix, with a fucked up emaciated Jesus, hung on the wall above the frame.

"Here it is. Please, hurry. The sun will be setting any time now. And you need to be out of the house by then." He opened the door. It creaked on rusty hinges. I saw a single flight of wooden steps led to the basement floor.

"Okay, Dr. Morrow. It will only take me a minute," I counted the steps on the way down. Each creaked and complained from the burden of supporting my weight. Thirteen steps to the basement floor, thirteen feet below.

As I stepped on each board, I felt the song gain strength. I could hear it as much as feel it with each foot I descended.

An epiphany came to me. He mentioned Margie, then he called her Margaret. Could the letters on the calendar be a menu? If so, 'M' is established as corned beef and cabbage. M could equal meat when you applied logic to the equation. What would 'P' and 'D's' favorite meals be? Poultry or pork for one, but the other?

I shined my flashlight down into the cellar. It illuminated the room. I found myself unprepared for the revelation. I swear to sweet Jesus the ghostly form of who I now assumed to be Margaret or Margie, Morrow hovered above the floor. Well, at least from the waist down. I jumped and almost slipped down the remaining steps.

By the time I tripped onto the floor, I caught a glimpse of her back, now turned to me, and her long blonde hair trailing down the middle of her back, tied in a ponytail. She moved to a smaller room in the back of the cellar.

I noted Dr. Morrow partially finished his basement. I expected nothing less from an engineer such as he. The neglected remains of a workshop flourished here. Most puzzling, though, at the center of it all stood a large centrifuge made of steel, chrome, and plastic.

Big enough for a pair of adults to stand inside, the machine stood motionless. Carbon scoring decorated the frame and a large section of the bottom lay twisted and melted. A large black mirror, anchored to a mahogany frame sat inside the device, partially covered by a drop cloth. As tall as a man and half as wide, the mirror captured the glare of my flashlight as I recovered my balance. A violet laser beam reflected off its surface, shooting toward the ghost.

I followed the beam's trajectory. The woman drifted away into the mudroom, seeming to flow with the melody of the song. She entered a small causeway and came to a dead end. Then she faded away before my eyes, revealing an astonishing sight. The song rose in volume, buzzing in the air around me.

Now I knew the melody. I felt it in my being, sending a chill up my spine. the song…

Along one wall, shelves built into the earth held speakers and pieces of a sound system. An old tube TV, the size of a computer monitor, stood on a tripod next to a mic stand. They stood in the corner and a thick patina of dirt covered all of it.

Opposite this, on the wall before me, stood what I could only call a shrine. A chrome rack held dozens of dried out, dead roses. Each laid in bunches. They filled the racks, except for the center. A basket in the center of the display contained the partially decomposed remains of a small animal. The remaining patches of fur did little to cover the animal's exposed skeleton. I guessed it died a decade or more ago.

"This mudroom was Margaret's favorite place in the house. She used to come here and sing, or if she wasn't singing she'd can vegetables, and store them on that rack," Dr. Morrow's sudden appearance failed to startle me this time. I knew he'd show up, "our wedding song was Dead Flowers from the Rolling Stones. She thought it was the most romantic song ever. So I buy her flowers every week, and when they die, I bring them down here. Her urn is next to her cat."

"That cat's seen better days," I said, followed by a nervous laugh. Morrow didn't reply. I saw the polished, wooden urn in the shadows. My heart broke inside for Dr. Morrow. He still loved his wife, whom tragedy stole from him so prematurely. I checked the wifi signal in the mudroom. The house's plaster and concrete blocked most of the transmitted radio waves.

"Well, what's the verdict?" Morrow asked.

"You're going to need a wifi booster down here, in the workshop in the cellar out there. Then you'll be fine. I've got one in my bag at the top of the stairs." I said and sped up the steps before the man could say another word. It occurred to me how brilliant this man might be, he couldn't figure out a simple wifi problem.

"Oh wonderful, and please, hurry. The sun, it's turning red." As I reached the threshold, crimson haze, the herald of dusk, shone through the kitchen windows, corroborating Morrow's words. The aroma of apples and pickling spices greeted me, hailing from the covered stockpot on the stove. Did I see her ghostly form standing before the stove, swaying to the beat of Charlie Watt's snare and high hat? Or did the steam play a trick on my eyes?

I believe the answer to both questions is…

Yes.

I dug into my bag and retrieved the signal booster. If my memory serves me, I believe when I turned my back the light in the kitchen turned to gray. I hurried down the stairs into the basement and went about installing the device. Another five minutes and Dr. Morrow would be happy. My track record for the day hit the shitter with another false assumption.

An alarm rang before I could do a thing. A series of beeps from somewhere inside the mudroom. It drove Morrow batshit on cue, soon as the sound started chirping away.

"Hurry, sir! You must hurry!" Dr. Morrow pleaded with me as he ran to the mudroom.

A loud bang stopped him in his tracks. It resonated through the basement. The makeshift lab's loose parts rattled in response. The gyroscope wobbled. The lights flickered.

"Oh, no. It's too late," Dr. Morrow managed to mutter. He fell to his knees, sniveling, before the shrine of dead flowers. An uncomfortable silence filled the basement. I noticed the song disappeared, too.

A second bang, with similar results. This time the sheet hanging from the mirror slipped off and fell to the floor. The silence continued.

Morrow put his quivering hands up to his ears. Tears streamed from his eyes, streamers of drool hung from his lips and chin. Unintelligible words streamed from his lips as he talked in tongues.

A third bang. The rack of dead roses moved. Something *behind* the display wanted out.

"You must leave! You must leave now! Come back tomorrow and finish the job! But go now!" Morrow pushed himself up from a knee and urged me up the stairs. I looked to the top and saw the ghostly figure of Margaret atop, standing at the door. She beckoned me, her brow furled and an expression of concern fell below it.

A louder bang, followed by a chaotic symphony of clanging metal, erupted. The rack and subsequently its contents blew forward and apart.

"Hurry, hurry. *Go.* Now! *Go! Before it's too late!*" Dr. Morrow frantically urged me on. I took three, leaping steps up the stairs, pulling myself up by the banister until I reached the top. I blew through the ghostly form of Mrs. Morrow in the process, her ethereal form dissipating in the act.

I slammed the door behind me, and locked it, shivering in fright and adrenaline, trying not to hyperventilate. In the adjoining kitchen, the aroma of the cooking dinner filled my senses, finally defeating the assault of the basement's stench. The ritual food Dr. Morrow cooked for the memory of his Margaret. Did he know his wife's spirit watched him make this?

I turned the stove off and took the bread out of the oven. I knew he'd get out, but not knowing the when of Morrow's inevitable escape from the cellar, it prompted me to take some pity on the crazy old doctor. His screaming from the cellar sent a chill through my bones.

A shimmering light hovered in the kitchen's window. It caught my attention. A glowing, ethereal hand-Margaret's hand-extended out from within me, and pulled me toward the light. I took it, giving myself to her intangible beauty. My vision warped with the twisting of reality. Something unseen pulled me away from the house and the occupants in the cellar of Dr. Morrow's creepy house. In the blink of an eye, I found myself sitting back in my work van shaking my head in denial.

Outside, I could still hear the doctor's lunatic screams echo in the night. The cries bouncing off the walls of his neighbors' homes, I sat for a few moments longer before asking my phone's digital DJ to play me some Rolling Stones. Dead Flowers appropriately came to life first, drowning out Dr. Morrow's wails.

What in the fuck did I witness in the home? A ghost in a mad scientist's house? Crazy Doc Morrow certainly held the trump card in the carnal carnival with his neighbors. He held it high over Papa John's Pill Popping Progeny and Bare Naked Coke Snorter. Shit, his house sat in the center of the big top, with all the spotlights shining upon it. And what does he get for a participation prize?

A golden achievement for the most fucked up shit in the cul de sac.

I signed off on the job, marking it incomplete with a return the next business day, on my tablet and drove away from Danforth Circle, into the night.

The evening to follow, like all the rest, sped by in a blur of motion. When I try to focus on it, bits and pieces of information flash by like a montage scene in a movie cut together by an editor on speed.

I don't have anyone to buy flowers for, but I grab a

dozen anyway at the gas station along my way. Next, I'm in my driveway, then I'm at my house. I put the roses on the table in my kitchen. I take a piss. I'm eating dinner, what I ate doesn't really matter. I don't remember. I do recall staring at the roses. I wash my face in the bathroom and look long and hard at my reflection in the medicine cabinet mirror. The other me in the glass shimmers, shifting in and out of focus, twisting my perception. My eyes see a different face, a feminine face, in the glass. Margaret's face. As soon as I recognize her features, the scene changes. I am sitting in the reclining chair, getting ready to watch TV.

I fall asleep and the night slowed it all the fuck down.

Cold embraces my legs, creeping up until my whole body shivers. But I don't wake, oh no. Someone, something, chooses to anesthetize me. Why? They know, much like a patient under the knife of surgery, I would writhe in agony if left to my own devices. They wish to make me privy to the horrible secrets they witnessed as a fly on the wall.

They experienced.

In spite of their preparations, I learned immediately nothing could desensitize me to what I would behold. A lavender pulsar flashed behind my closed eyes, opening them in another mind. The images flickered through the filter of an old reel to reel projector on the mental screen.

Nothing could prepare for the madness to follow…

Fractured visions, warped by the glass of the windows in my mind. A centrifuge rotates, emanating prismatic light and blasting kaleidoscopic images. All of this intermixed with the steady rhythm of an EKG and hum of fluorescent hospital lights.

A centrifuge completes a rotation in one direction and shifts the view. A black mirror twinkles with light. A girl walking a dog in a park. Another rotation, another shift. The same woman singing karaoke at a smoke-filled bar, but some years older. Yet one more rotation welcomes one more shift. The same lady, now old and weeping, brushing her graying hair.

And in between each shift, a shimmer, bathed in silver and gold brilliance. A lone, pale figure, singing a song as pure as the light itself.

Margaret…

I woke in the morning refreshed. The images from this dream burned into my memory. The Doctor Michael Morrow of today didn't deserve to have his wife back. Margaret belonged to someone who loved her, and her alone.

The following day saw me ignoring my other scheduled appointments and returning to Danforth Circle.

Why shouldn't I?

I needed to finish my work…

The closer I got to Danforth Circle, the louder their song grew in volume, until I stepped onto the property. The melody engulfed me, resonating through my flesh and bones. The old man took his time answering the door. I raised my hand to knock again when he opened the door. Dr. Morrow looked like shit. A dark bruise stood out on the top of his head. Black bags set under his eyes.

"It's about time. How long will this take? Not long, I hope."

"No, not long, I was almost done last night."

"Good, good. I have something to attend to upstairs. I'll be right back. If you need me in the interim, call out."

"I sure will," I replied and watched the man scurry away through the mildewed boxes. I wondered if I interrupted his morning constitutional. It didn't matter. I went directly to the basement.

A chaos I can only assume resembled the Tazmanian Devil of Looney Tunes fame struck the cellar. The booster I left here the night before moved. To where I couldn't see. My search brought me into the remains of Dr. Morrow's lab and the centrifuge. The slipcover on the black mirror now lay in a clump on the floor, the cloth flowing around the wi-fi booster.

The mirror appeared to be made of a single sheet of black volcanic glass. It sat in a mahogany frame, built to house the obsidian. Cracks from a blow formed a splintered circle in the upper corner. I detected a movement behind me in the mirror. I turned around and saw nothing except a white tile wall. Shaking my head, I bent over to pick up the booster. I rose to see the image of Mrs. Morrow floating in the mirror. Our reflections melded together as I stood.

And my soul bonded with another.

The mirror's scene changes from a basement lab to a hospital room. Bright fluorescent lights sit on the ceiling above me, illuminating the room. I hear the steady hum of a ventilator pushing air in and out of my lungs. It's a driving rhythm, setting the tone for the steady beeping of an EKG Monitor, its wires and tubes attached to my arms and face. The machines are a two-man backup band, and, and the soft dripping of the morphine in the bag attached to a vein in my wrist is the lead singer.

Cancer sucks. Dying from it sucks for those you leave behind. Without warning, the EKG flatlines, releasing a steady, alarming tone. I don't feel a thing as I close my eyes. When I open them, I'm floating above the body in the light. I see Margaret Morrow, there, in the bed, her long silver hair matted with sweat as the cancer ate her body away.

I realize my name isn't Jeff Andrews anymore. It's Margaret Daisy Morrow. And I have bore witness to travesties unheard of.

The door to the ICU room opens, nurses run in. There is a brief attempt to revive me. It fails. Moments later he dashes into the room. Dr. Michael Morrow, a brilliant scientist, does not hide the distress in his heart. He is distraught, screaming in pain and loss. High school sweethearts, the couple spent decades together in the flesh. And though he obsessed with his work, he also doted on her every single day as if he courted her for the first time.

Then Margaret died.

It's this last decade where the relationship became one-sided. The ghost she became could watch, but it could not stop the man she loved from spiraling into madness.

Mike never officially quit F-LAB. He never came back after his bereavement leave. Instead, he spent his days and nights building the gyroscope in the basement. Followed by an equally proportionate number of months calculating the equations for it to work.

Then came the trip to South America, and the obsidian mirror, the focus key for everything to work. Purchased for a large sum of money from a black market dealer, all of this unfolded like an adventure in and of itself. But gunfights with pirates, a witch's curse, and the sacrifice of his sanity could not be compared to the bullshit Mike planned for his endgame.

The black mirror. In combination with the contraption he built around it, and the calculations he spent years perfecting, it became a nexus of time within a confined space. The device would allow him to create a wormhole within the mirror and step through the quantum barrier. His goal? To comb through infinite, alternate earths.

Filled with infinite, alternate Margarets.

He handpicked them, one by one. Of all ages until he possessed a three-faced goddess representing his wife at different stages of her life. Crone, Mother, and Maiden.

He built them a home within a bunker dug outside under the guise of an inground swimming pool. He laid an eight-foot by twenty-four-foot cargo container within and covered it with a mound of dirt. Access to the bunker came through a fifteen-foot tunnel connecting the basement's mudroom to the secret chamber. A small box on top held a hatch cover in place, and a three-rung ladder dropped into the bunker. Mike sealed this tunnel with a steel compression door. Only he could open it. The new

Margaret would need to live here, to be conditioned, re-educated on where she now lived.

And I beheld it all as they experienced it before…

Margie Morrow sat on the edge of her bed brushing her hair. She dragged the brush through her tresses, wincing when she caught a snag. Gray strands peppered her blonde. Across the room, the mirror on her dresser reflected her image.

The mirror shimmered and at first, Margie thought her eyes played tricks on her. As it widened, spreading out like a pond after the impact of a stone. The waves reached the frame and shook the whole dresser.

"Mike?" She called out to her husband. "Was there an earthquake? Mike?" Margie stood up and cautiously walked to her dresser. The mirror appeared to have returned to normal, "Mike, can you hear me?" She heard a shuffling of chairs in the kitchen, downstairs. The distant voice of her husband answered with mumbled unintelligible words. "I can't hear you, honey, come upstairs if you can hear me!"

"I'm already here. I can hear you just fine, Margaret."

"You know I hate being called Margaret, Mike," She admonished her husband and turned her head to the doorway to the bedroom.

No one. She remained alone in the room.

"Mike?" She turned her head left and right, looking all about the room. Sweat beaded on her forehead and she shook in fear. A stillness took over the moment. Margie stood up.

Two arms reached out from inside the mirror, grabbed her by the shoulders in a vice grip of steel, and Margie lifted off the ground. The shock of the moment stilled Margie's tongue for half a breath. A moment long enough for the abductor to pull Margie out of her reality before she could kick, fight, or scream for help.

Flaring, hypnotizing lights shot forth from a kaleidoscope. Then light erupted into a void of black…

A country lick played out of a pair of loudspeakers in the basement of the Morrow house. Peggy Morrow stood in the karaoke room, or rather mudroom in the basement. A complete setup existed in the basement of the house, fourteen-inch speakers, an eight hundred watt power amp/mixing board hybrid, a flat-screen monitor on a cart, and a wireless mic nestled on a stand.

She cranked the Rolling Stones and sang Dead Roses at the top of her lungs. A pair of cushioned, high back chairs, upholstered in red silk, made for luxurious accommodations in the root cellar.

The song started skipping.

"What the fuck," Peggy let out a rare F-bomb. The lights in the basement flickered. "This can't be good." The floorboards above her head rattled. Dust sifted down in the flickering light. "An earthquake?" She whispered.

Peggy sat up from one of the chairs and set to turn off the electronics. She touched the mixing board and a shock of electricity threw her back into the chair. Her face froze in a snarl. Her short, blonde hair stood out straight, giving her the look of a pissed off punk rocker. Dazed, she couldn't move, but she could see everything going on around her.

The monitor came to life, the only light in the darkness. The screen paused on a close-up of Mick Jagger's lips.

"Hello, Margaret," the lips said.

"My name is Peggy," she found the gift of speech returned to her, "Mike? Why in the fuck would you be using that name with me?"

"Of course it is," he paused, "Margaret."

Peggy watched, helpless, as the lips grew larger, expanding from the TV screen. She wanted to scream as Mick's mouth engulfed her, but she couldn't. Instead, she watched as her body fell through a series of pixelated rainbows, bending and stretching. An aether net held her within its confines, pulling her through a dozen different realities…

Daisy Ames walked her dogs through the village of Fenton, alongside Lake Ontario, into parks, and across sidewalks, the teenager led a pair of mutts, one small and shaggy, the other medium-sized with a short coat. They sniffed and trotted with Daisy following up behind them.

The trio came to a park. A small pond sat in the middle, next to a white, wicker gazebo. Daisy found a stone bench at the water's side. The sun reflected off the pond's surface and onto Daisy, cascading across her young frame.

She hummed a song she heard on the radio earlier today, mumbling the melody. The song echoed across the pond, skipping across the water like a flat rock. A pair of geese swimming in the pond squawked, honked and flew off. Daisy stopped humming.

"Sorry I scared you off," she said to the geese. At least her dogs, Dusty and Petunia, ignored the geese. The animals laid in the grass at Daisy's feet.

The growling of the dogs broke her from her daydreaming. Petunia, a pitbull lab mix, rarely showed her teeth. But both she and her little brother Dusty growled and snarled in full guard dog mode at this moment.

"What is it?" Daisy asked them. Petunia tugged on her leash so hard she broke loose of Daisy's grip. The mutt sped off after something unseen by the gazebo. Dusty tried to join his companion but caught whiplash as the leash went taught. The little dog squeaked as he did a backflip and landed on his side. Daisy got up and chased after Petunia, Dusty running at her side.

"Tuney!" The girl shouted for her dog as she ran to the gazebo at the water's edge. When she arrived, she stopped in her tracks. An old man, with his back to Daisy, stood behind the gazebo. He held Petunia's leash. Dusty stopped with his master, opting to yip a warning at the man.

"Margaret?" The man asked as he turned around.

"Nobody calls me Margaret unless I'm in trouble or they're a substitute teacher," Daisy said, "and I don't think you're a sub."

"Is this Petunia?" He said, "Lord, I haven't seen–"

"How do you know my dog's name?" Her eyes grew wide in fear.

"Just a lucky guess. I guess," the man stood, fully revealed, albeit his face masked. Middle-aged, balding with a ragged salt and pepper beard covering his face, the hairs poking out from underneath his mask.

"Do… I know you?" Daisy asked him.

"No," he paused, "well, that's not true. You know *a* me, but not *this* me." He stepped toward her. She stepped away.

"I don't get what you are saying. Who are you?"

"Someone who loves you very much, Margaret." He released the dog. Petunia ran past Daisy, putting as much space between it and the man as the dog could.

"It's okay, I've got you, baby!" The man exclaimed and lunged forward.

"Baby?" Daisy screamed, "I'm nobody's baby!" Determined to not be a victim of a random stalker, Daisy tried to sidestep the man, but the spread of his arms still caught her.

The man grabbed the teenager in a bear hug. He squeezed the air out of her lungs and she dropped Dusty's leash. The mutt yipped once. The old man kicked Dusty, sending the little dog spinning across the grass. Then he covered her mouth with a rag, cutting off her supply of air. She kicked and punched, but the old man out matched her. Daisy stopped fighting, she no longer possessed the strength. Instead, she watched the unbelievable unfold before her eyes.

The man lifted her up and threw her over his shoulder. He walked into the pond. The landscape shifted. From the underwater kingdom of the pond to a rainbow arcing over an infinite mountain range, into a bank of clouds.

A chaotic orchestra of insanity brought me out of my trance…

"What are you doing in there?" Dr. Morrow screamed. I still stood within the centrifuge, grasping the wifi booster. For how long, I couldn't be sure. I felt their song, the reassuring melody calmed my nerves.

These visions of women being abducted plagued my mind's eye. And now I knew the answer to the riddle of the letters. They belonged to Dr. Morrow's victims. Margie, Peggy, and Daisy, by the first initial. What he did with them to require an initial, made part of me wonder. I'd find out soon enough.

A part of me once felt pity for this desperate man. The rest of me knew he needed to fuck off. After what he did to these women and what his actions caused them to become, he took despicable to a new level. This house, this whole place, it mirrored the ruins of a lost wizard's castle in a D&D game. And Dr. Michael Morrow fancied himself the Dungeon Master in this adventure.

"The booster, it was over here. Quite the mess you've got."

"Stay away from that thing, it's dangerous. What did you see in your reflection?"

"Nothing," I said out loud, *right? I saw nothing?* I said to myself. What did I see in the mirror?

"Is this fixed, this thing? Is your work done here?"

"Yeah, yeah it is," I replied, shaking as I showed him the meter on the booster, "see?"

"Good, now get out of my house."

"It'll be my pleasure." Before I could step out of the gyroscope, the lights in the cellar extinguished.

"Nice." I said.

"Shut up, you fool!" Dr. Morrow ordered me, "they'll hear you! Oh, God, please no!" I heard him skitter away. The light of a cell phone illuminated a halo around Morrow. The shadows bounced off his features, giving him a sinister appearance. He fumbled with an app. Something beeped. "Oh God, oh no."

"What is it?" I asked.

A scraping and hissing replied from somewhere within the cellar.

"Pray to God they don't want to keep you!"

"Who in the fuck are you talking about?"

"My Margarets!" He screamed in anguish.

The song grew in volume, but it sounded different.

It lost its ethereal presence. The vocalists now stood in the room within proximity of me and Dr. Morrow. He wept in time to the song's melody. The singing grew in volume and intensity. The temperature dropped. It became apparent something, or somethings, joined in the room.

Out of the void, something cold and wet wrapped around my waist and pulled me out of the gyroscope. I slammed into the tile floor, jamming my shoulder blade and ribs. Vices of ice clasped on my legs as a caressing tendril pressed into my temple.

Their soothing song continued on. Ice cold hands held me down on the floor in the darkness of the cellar. The stench of something putrid lingered in the air. The door above me crashed open. Some unseen force blowing it open. A fresh blast of air, scented with apples, accompanied the light invading the darkness. The song abruptly stopped. I saw a trio of blind, hairless, white-skinned creatures cowering in the dark, hissing, and snarling.

They may have once been human. The paradox of reality changed them. Now these creatures, not of our world, once human and now transformed into something else more hideous than a sane person could fathom. This plane of existence didn't welcome them here, and thus our reality rejected them as your body might reject a toxin, a virus, or an organ transplant.

The light grew from the opening. I saw the ghost of Margaret Morrow standing strong and determined at the top of the stairs. A frown covered her face.

"Margaret?" I heard Dr. Morrow say. I saw him step

between myself and the creatures he imprisoned. "Is that really you, Margaret?"

The ghost nodded. And closed her eyes. Dr. Morrow wept.

"I'm so sorry. So, so sorry." Dr. Morrow said as he cried. The trio of creatures continued to hiss. "Shut up! Oh shut up all of you!"

Then we heard it.

The song. Her song…

Their song.

Dead Flowers…

The Ghost of Margaret Morrow floated in the air and sang her song… *their song.* A Banshee cry, lamenting and forlorn, it spread through the basement and those within its confines. The creatures, or what remained of these beings from other Earths, shrieked in terror, along with Dr. Morrow. He covered his ears with his hands. His victims skittered away, retreating to their hidden bunker hidden behind the wall of the mudroom.

"No, no it can't be! No. I watched you die in the hospice! I did all of this to bring you back, but you were here the whole time? Oh, my sweet, sweet Margaret. Don't you know I would have never done any of this had I known you were here?" Dr. Morrow's tone changed from scared to angry. "Why didn't you tell me? I braved the cosmos. I took things from beings who live in pockets of time and are still looking to retrieve the secrets I stole from them. I stepped through hell and back to find you, and all I could find was *other* you's. Not *quite* you. And look at what they became!" He pointed to the creatures, who once had names, and lives, and futures in their own realities.

The pitiful, warped creatures, once human with families and names. And the ghost of Margaret Morrow promised to remind her widower of his sin.

Do you remember Margie? The Banshee wailed, *Who didn't die of cancer in her world? Her Mike wasn't crazy, but he did spend more time with his work than he did with his wife. You didn't know the fine-tuning of this damned device, and your inexperience traveling through the multiverse. You could see her through the mirror and you watched her for weeks before finally reaching in and grabbing her.*

"Why do you remind me of these evils? I'm already damned by what remains of them!"

Or poor, poor Peggy who tried to save all of them!

"And ended up being the one to damn them! She never should have touched the Device!" He pointed to the gyroscope and mirror.

You thought a Margaret in her prime would suffice, perhaps she would be more open. You made your mind up when the mirror showed you a Margaret singing our wedding song. She stole your breath and you stole Peggy from the mudroom of her house, one very similar to mine. This time the wormhole sent you through the glass of a television on the other end. The curve of the glass distorted both travelers.

Peggy would not be the solution to the problem. In fact, she became the most difficult to deal with. The most rebellious. The most dangerous. She hated being called Margaret. Whereas Margie let it slide, Peggy wouldn't. She would become violent, attacking you, punching and kicking. How often did you find yourself forced into sedating Peggy, leaving her in the dungeon for days?

He didn't answer. Tears welled in his eyes, snot dripped from his nose.

And Daisy. After watching her for months, you stepped through the mirror and entered Daisy's world. You hoped she might recognize you as her love. After all, during this time, your teenage self dated this Margaret in the same manner you courted me. But when she tried to run, you forced himself on young Daisy, drugging her before carrying her back through the barrier.

"I never touched her, I'm not a pedophile!"

Not until she came of age.

Peggy's escape attempt put a kibosh to those plans and spelled the ultimate demise of herself and your other victims. Peggy cracked the black mirror in an effort to use the gyroscope to return to her own reality.

The crack changed the others. They became spoiled, like leftovers hidden in the back of a refrigerator for a decade. They molded, rotted and festered until nothing left resembled Margie, Peggy, or Daisy. The things hid during the day, living in the bunker out of practical choice, lamenting their damnation with the song.

The trio of creatures writhed in pain from the light, twisting away from it, hiding in the shadows. All the same person. All individuals in their own right. Now they mutated, transformed into corruptions of their former selves. The ghost of Margaret Morrow sent this message to her husband and continued to sing her favorite song from the Rolling Stones as she floated to the top of the stairs.

And there they are now, all trapped together with Michael Morrow, all of the Margarets of his life, condemned to this house. To protect them from inquiring eyes, Dr. Morrow sealed the entrance to the dungeon and placed its lock on a time-release, using the wifi. He lets them out at night and feeds them what he calls boiled dinner. Most days it's the remains of roadkill, boiled with spices. They lost their sense of taste long ago.

Now I know after dinner is when the fun begins. *Their* fun. They have their way with Michael Morrow… satisfying their carnal delights through unspeakable acts of perversion, breaking taboos unknown by the mortal men of this reality. This would have been my fate, Jeff Andrews, to join her husband in this damnation. I could not let this happen. Unlike her husband, who spent his days abducting her from other realities, I have greater foresight.

He never once took to the notion his wife might be watching his every move. If he did, if the scientist in him allowed him to believe in the possibilities of ghosts for a moment, things may have been different. A simple re-calibration of his device would have opened a doorway to the other side, where he would find the Margaret he loved waiting for him.

And what about me? The lone observer of this tragedy?

I fell in love with a ghostly song…

A flood of emotion surged. Unconditional love. It filled my body with elation, filling my soul with joy.

Emotions like love are difficult to interpret. I became more than infatuated with the ghost of Margaret Morrow and her song…

Our song.

Inspired, I took advantage of the moment the ghost of Margaret Morrow provided me, and launched up the stairs. The lights from the kitchen caught the black mirror within the centrifuge. The surface reflected back, as it did before. Violet lasers of light ricocheted off the floor and ceiling of the cellar, then up the stairs. I stepped through the spirit of the doctor's wife as the lasers struck both the tangible and the incorporeal at once. Her form dissipated as the purple light pulsated. A chill shot up my spine and stole my breath as I left the house.

I got in my van, drove away from Danforth Circle, and took the rest of the day off.

A week ago all of this happened. One single week. Seven fucking days. And here I am now, with my ear to the ground, listening to you sing along with your corrupted sisters, all while a bastard laments his evil acts and waits for his next night of hellish orgies with creatures from beyond. Our song is there. I hear you singing through the ground, calling me back to the house, to put an end to all of this. As much as I'd like to, I can't say if, or when, I will oblige.

Today?

Tomorrow?

Next week?

How long can I control the urges? To do what I should do and what Dr. Morrow never thought to do? I get back into my van and drive off. Sticky Fingers picks up where it left off. Life is good if you accept the lie. The sun is shining, and Mick reminds me it sure can be a bitch.

Before I get home, I stop at a convenience store on the way and buy a dozen roses. When I finally get back to my driveway, I park my van and go over to my pick-up truck. I check the glove compartment. The red box full of shotgun shells is where I put it. The pump-action twelve-gauge sits on the gun rack behind my head. It's not pretty, but it is an effective pest control device, regardless of the vermin's origin. If it bleeds, it can die.

My tools are all set in the back. Who knows when the urge to play with an eclectic erector set may come upon me. An arc welder, drills, wiring gauges, fuses, and everything else I might need to repair a mad scientist project.

Satisfied, I leave the truck. Instead of the house, I go straight to the garage. Inside, hanging from the rafters, are bunches of dead, dehydrated roses. I hang the new bouquet with the dozen or so others crisscrossing the ceiling of the garage. Soon I'll have an itchy trigger finger…

And enough roses to refill a rack.

AGAINST THE GRAIN

Hello, Jessica, I love you. A day doesn't go by where I don't think about you. Ever since you were born I've cherished you. I know I haven't been there for everything, but I can promise you this will change. I've got so many regrets, things I want to make up to you. Going forward, I'll be the one person you can rely on. Why? Because I gave birth to you and this is the least I can do. It's what I'm supposed to do.

"I'm your mother," Courtney DeJulio said aloud, punctuating the rant, before starting over. The words repeated in Courtney's head. Each sentence raced in tandem with the mile markers and cow pastures lining the interstate.

"I am your mother," she looked at her reflection in the rearview mirror and watched how her lips articulated, how she spoke the words. Courtney knew her body language needed to match the sincerity in her heart.

"If you only knew what I did for you, dear daughter, the sacrifices I made for you." She watched as dusk settled on the horizon behind her. Before her, the white stripes of the highway reflected the lights of Courtney's vehicle. Each created a translucent, hovering specter on the rural road.

The dancing ghosts disappeared when another pair of headlights grew from the oncoming horizon. High-set and bright, they filled the road with light, forcing Courtney to shield her eyes as her SUV closed the distance between them. Photo negative dots filled her vision and the long, droopy sleeve of her sweater came close to blocking her sight.

"Dick head!" She flashed her brights and a moment later the vehicle, a tractor-trailer hauling a trailer full of Lord-knows-what, dimmed its lights. "Gee, thanks!" She laid the full force of her palm into the horn on her steering wheel as the truck sped closer.

Oh, no. She mouthed the words without speaking when she saw the doe jump out in front of the truck.

A tractor with a fully loaded trailer weighs in at just under forty tons. A female ungulate will tip the scales at approximately one hundred pounds. An eighty thousand pound mallet struck the deer. In a fraction of time, say, the amount of it required to blink, a living, breathing organism ceased to exist.

An explosion of red filled the road, spraying Courtney's windshield in gore. She heard a loud bang as something struck the hood of her SUV. Courtney threw both hands on the wheel and yanked it to the right, hoping to avoid any residual damage from the deer or truck.

The SUV drove onto the shoulder as the tractor-trailer barreled on through. Courtney slammed on the brake, bringing the vehicle to a skidding stop in the roadside gravel.

She let out a sigh of relief, shifted the SUV into park, and rolled down the window for some fresh air. She could see more deer in the herd now crossing the road. She wondered if they knew what happened to the doe. Did the truck create an orphan? When the herd all crossed, a half dozen deer in total, and her heart rate slowed down a bit, Courtney decided the time was right for her to move on.

Gore covered the windshield. She flicked on the windshield wipers. A single wipe cleaned the window but left pink and red streaks. The wipers revealed more than a clear view.

"Jesus Christ!" Courtney screamed out loud.

Resting on the hood, a half-crushed deer's head stared at the woman with one eye intact. The creature's lips were peeled back, revealing a jester's grin full of twisted and bent teeth.

She put the SUV in drive and floored it, kicking up gravel and throwing it into the air behind her. The tires propelled the vehicle onto the road. She straightened the wheels, and the deer head slid off the hood as the SUV sped away.

It took a few miles for her heart rate and breathing to settle.

The GPS alerted Courtney to her nearby destination, advising her to exit the toll road. Weeks before, she reserved a night at a country Bed and Breakfast. The woman preferred intimate lodging, making this the perfect resting spot for a weary traveler on the go.

If she could rest.

Hours later, tossing and turning in an unfamiliar bed, Courtney resolved she and sleep weren't going to agree this night. The visual of the deer's decapitated head added to the dilemma. She couldn't close her eyes without seeing it staring back at her. Not to mention, going to see her daughter always troubled her.

Each year, without fail, whenever the trip came, anxiety knocked on her door. Like a champ, Courtney took one for the team and let the demon in. Rapid-fire thoughts spewed from the devil's lips. All of the things she might say to Jessica log-jammed in her mind and kept her awake.

Things she'll never say.

"I'm your mother," Courtney whispered, pulling the sheets off her body. A freak October heatwave made matters worse. The higher than normal temperature and accompanying humidity made any blanket or sheet useless. She wondered if the bed and breakfast left the heat on.

Courtney determined the windows weren't open wide enough to catch a breeze. She hopped out of the bed, naked. The thought of anything fabric touching her flesh at this moment made her feel hotter. With both arms, Courtney pushed one of the room's two windows up.

It overlooked the front of the Bed and Breakfast. Outside, a gentle wind rattled the chains holding the property's lavish sign. Giant letters, written in boisterous calligraphy, Christened the joint 'Stormy Hollow'. She could feel a cold breeze enter the room, cooling her flesh as it did.

"Thank God!" Courtney said. Then she realized her tits were hanging out for the whole world to see. The cool air stiffened her nipples and sent a chill through her bones. The woman covered her breasts up with her arms and walked to the other window. The undersides of her arms, rough with scar tissue from years of trying to feel pain, made her boobs itch. This time she stood to the side, used the linen curtain to cover her chest, and raised the window with one arm.

Courtney sighed in relief for doing so. The window overlooked the forested lot behind the bed and breakfast. The old rectory house rested on a burm lined with wheel ruts, between two hills. The full moon lit the night up, and Courtney could see much of the back, clear as day.

She heard something outside. A mewing whine, like an animal crying in pain. Her heart jumped when her eyes registered movement and she pulled the curtain tighter to her body.

Down this path, a lone woman walked. Dressed in a nightshirt with her head cocked to the right and covered by a shawl, the lady carried an empty tray in her hands. The woman's white dress radiated too brightly in the moonlight, blurring her face when the shawl might reveal her visage.

The way she moved didn't appear to be normal. It looked as if she floated over the hilly terrain. All of this seemed odd to Courtney, something altogether unnatural.

"Son of a bitch," she whispered. The hairs on her nape rose, she felt her heartbeat increase. Is that a fucking ghost? The thought lingered in her head until the figure's path removed it from Courtney's line of sight. She stuffed the curtain under her armpits and stuck her head out of the window.

Courtney's enthusiasm took a tumble as she only found disappointment. No ghost woman. The trees and hills stood and rolled, respectively, but no one, alive or spectral, walked through them. She shrugged her shoulders and walked away from the window.

Courtney used the bathroom and retrieved a satchel from her overnight bag. She brought the package back to bed with her, sat on the edge of the mattress, and withdrew its contents. Courtney grasped in her hand a stack of greeting cards and ragged newspaper clippings. She fanned through them, each card featured a cat of some sort in its art. She opened the one on top, a sad-faced kitten adorned the cover. Inside it read, in a child's broken script, "Love you, mommy. JESSICA" next to the factory inscription "MISSING YOU!"

Courtney cried as she sorted through the pile of cards. In minutes the room cooled down. Courtney laid back down clutching the stack of cards. This time, fatigue and emotion overcame her demons and deer skulls. She fell asleep.

Morning greeted the guests of Stormy Hollow with the aroma of a country breakfast. It lured the guests to the dining room. Now Courtney sat at the dining table with a couple, two other guests, and the proprietor, Patsy Chapman.

Nearing middle-age, Patsy used brown dye to keep the gray out, but her mop of curls was starting to lose the battle. Her attire screamed Hippy, with a wardrobe full of tye-dye sundresses and flip flops, which she wore through all four seasons.

Nobody engaged with anyone, instead, they focused on their breakfasts. The meal consisted of the usual fare: eggs, bacon, sausage, toast, fruit, and so forth. The couple drank smoothies. Mrs. Chapman drank a Bloody Mary out of the blender with a straw. Raising her coffee for a sip, Courtney broke the ice.

"Someone is going to have a good day."

"You're telling me, honey," the proprietor replied, "it's the secret to my success. Aren't you hot in that sweater? I know it's October, but it's already seventy-five degrees out."

"I don't pay too much attention to the weathermen or the news. I probably should. I've been making this trip for sixteen years now, and this is the first October heatwave I can remember."

"Ain't that the truth, honey. So you're on your way to visit your daughter in Fenton?" Patsy asked Courtney.

"Yes, I do it every year. Going on I don't know, sixteen

of them now? Something like that. I drive all the way from the Poconos."

"Wow, that's some miles," another sip of the Bloody Mary followed, "can't say I miss having an empty nest. Any grandkids?"

"Oh, no. I hope not. She's still in high school."

"I didn't think you looked old enough to be a gramma, but you never know nowadays."

"No gray hairs. Yet. Heck, I'm only turning thirty for the third time this year. I was young when I had her, she," Courtney paused for a moment, smiled, then found the word she wanted to use, "she lives with her father." The women laughed together, even getting a few of the diners to join in the revelry, which lasted until Courtney continued, "So who else saw the ghost last night?"

Silverware tinged on porcelain plates and the room went silent.

"Ghost?" Patsy asked after a few uncomfortable moments, "Are you crazy? No, dear, we don't have any ghosts at Stormy Hollow. They attract weirdos. They're not good for business at a Bed and Breakfast, all you get is stinky people sweating up your linens."

"You're kidding, right? I saw it, last night, in your backyard. A lady in white."

"A lady in white?" A smile grew on the woman's face, "Of course you didn't," Patsy guffawed at her wordplay and slapped her thigh.

"I'm being serious, I saw a ghost in your backyard last night." The other breakfast diners broke their silence.

Mumbled whispers were exchanged. Though she couldn't make out the words, Courtney knew they talked about her.

"Let me guess, it came from the old cemetery over a lot," Patsy let out a belly laugh. The other diners followed suit.

"This makes sense. I didn't know there was a cemetery nearby."

"Now you know and it shouldn't make any sense." Patsy stopped laughing long enough to take a big sip from her bloody Mary. The leaves on the celery stalk tickled her nose and she almost sneezed. She squinted her eyes and shook her head. "That wouldn't have been good. Listen, ghosts aren't real. You really don't believe in that mumbo jumbo, do you? It was probably a reflection from the highway."

"Well, no. This is the first time I've seen a ghost, to be honest. But I'm sure I saw one." Courtney remained firm on conviction, knowing what she saw was no reflection.

"I don't think you are listening to me. You didn't see a ghost." Patsy rose the giant Bloody Mary to her lips and took another sip.

"No. I'm sure I saw a ghost. A lady in white with a tray–"

"You don't give up, do you," Patsy interrupted, shaking her head, a scowl on her face. The diners stopped talking. Patsy dropped her drink to the floor. The blender shattered on the stone tile flooring, sending glass and ice flying while covering anyone near Patsy in tomato juice and vodka.

Things you can't unsee.

Courtney stared at the mess, unable to take her eyes away. The alcohol and juice formed a perfect puddle around Patsy. It reminded Courtney of the deer hitting the truck.

Things you'll never forget.

The bottom of the blender mixer lay in a pile of ice and glass Patsy's feet. She shifted her leg and a shadow fell across the remains. It grabbed Courtney's attention. Her heart pounded in her chest.

Is that a deer's head?

"Everyone out!" Patsy screamed, throwing her hands in the air. She lost her patience in the same manner her hair lost its battle with the gray.

Courtney broke from her trance and, with everyone else, left as ordered. Fifteen minutes later, she took her bag and checked out of Stormy Hollow. She drove away in her SUV, hoping never to see a ghost again.

She wouldn't be so fortunate.

The grounds of Oak Run cemetery spread over acres, creating a serene oasis in the middle of the dying city of Fenton. Courtney drove the SUV in, looking for the spot she liked to park in. She hoped to God she wouldn't crash any funerals this day. Her prayers were answered when she discovered there were none.

Courtney hated funerals.

She came upon a large, marble and granite mausoleum.

Next to the tomb, an empty space large enough to fit a vehicle revealed itself. Courtney smiled and parked the SUV in the spot. She turned off the ignition and sighed.

Now the waiting game began, languishing for the right time, the right moment to approach her daughter. To do things the right way for once. With it, came the mantra, reminding her of things she'll never say.

"I'm your mother," Courtney said aloud and forced a smile while she watched… and waited.

Butterflies invaded her belly when she saw a pair of figures, dressed in black and holding hands, standing before a gravestone. The smaller of the two bent down and placed something on the ground. Courtney sat up, trying to get a better view, but she couldn't. Too many trees and branches obscured her line of sight. She straightened her clothing and exited the SUV. By the time Courtney rounded the side of the mausoleum, the figures were walking away.

No, Jessica! I'm your mother! She wanted to shout out, but couldn't.

Courtney's heart sank. She ran, avoiding headstones and markers. She reached the spot they had stood at, but she could no longer see them. The pair disappeared, around a hill. Looking down, Courtney saw a card with a grumpy cat on the front, sitting on a grave surrounded by flowers in different states of life and death.

Courtney didn't need to read the inscription on the gravestone. She knew the words written on it. They remained unchanged for the last sixteen years:

VALERIE D. FISCHER –
BELOVED WIFE AND MOTHER
JULY 7, 1967 – OCTOBER 30, 2004

But now it sat alongside two empty graves:

ROBERT J. FISCHER
1965 –
JESSICA A. FISCHER
1999 –

Courtney picked up the card. The factory print read: *I'm grumpy because I can't hug you!* Then she read its handwritten contents:

> *Dear Mom,*
> *Dad and I miss you, every day. I wish I could see you, hold you. I turned 21 this year, so he told me the truth, of how I'm adopted. He was afraid it would change how I feel about him, how I feel about you. But nothing's changed. Dad thought I might want to find my biological mom, but I don't see the point.*
> *I know I only have vague memories of you, of who you were, but I want to remember them and I want to remember you as my Mom, not some stranger who gave me up because they got pregnant when they were thirteen.*
> *I hate cancer.*

> *Dad bought new plots for both of us to*
> *be buried with you when the Lord calls us.*
> *We hope you don't mind. We miss you. We*
> *love you.*
> *Your daughter, forever.*
> *Jessica*

In silence, Courtney took the card and walked away from the grave, back to her SUV. Nothing raced through her mind, the moment transformed it into a senseless void, empty of thought or emotion. She opened the trunk, retrieved the satchel of greeting cards and clippings, added one more card to the stack, and put it away. She closed the trunk, opened the driver's door, and sat in the seat. For hours she stared at nothing, said nothing.

Thought nothing.

Soon, dusk came to Oak Run cemetery, the blazing red of the setting sun burned through the gaps in the trees, and found a target. The glare broke Courtney from her catatonic state, blinding her. Sunspots swirled in her vision, disorienting her, reminding her of the tractor-trailer and the deer. A vision of the deer skull filled her mind. She closed her eyes and shook her head, but the vision wouldn't go away as long as they remained closed.

Courtney opened her eyes and dealt with the setting sun. She saw something flicker in the trees. She squinted, and in the distance, something moved, something otherworldly, rising with the evening fog. Someplace an animal in distress mewed, causing Courtney to shiver in fear.

The glowing haze approached an open parcel of land and Courtney wanted to shit her pants. The ghostly lady in white, still carrying an empty tray, walking in the cemetery. The apparition moved with a purpose. It glided through headstones and past the grave of Val Fischer, the woman who pretended to be a mother to Courtney's daughter.

Toward the SUV.

"Fuck this," Courtney cursed. She turned the ignition, put the SUV in reverse, back out, and drove off, putting distance between her and the specter. She hit the main road and pressed the accelerator to the floor, hitting eighty miles per hour on Rt 104 as she streaked away from the Oak Run cemetery and Fenton, New York.

The Stormy Hollow Bed and Breakfast's NO VACANCY sign lit up the front window of the old rectory house. Courtney didn't care, she wasn't going there, specifically. Behind it, maybe, but not to it. She drove past the hostel and down a country road, looking for the mystery cemetery Patsy mentioned the day before.

It didn't take long to find it, off the side of the road. The small, regional graveyard laid out next to a four-pew white church, complete with a steeple. A folding placard in front of the church declared Stormy Hollow Chapel. Courtney parked next to the place of worship, turned the phone's flashlight on, and grabbed her traveling day bag from the back seat.

Wisps of fog floated in the air, making it difficult to see, even with a light. But she found a comfortable spot in the cemetery and sat down. Her back leaned against a limestone gravestone, its letters faded by weather and time.

Courtney emptied the contents of her traveling bag onto the grass. A change of clothes, miscellaneous toiletries, and the satchel full of memories lay before her, closed tight. Inside it, the sins of a teenager remained hidden, festering. The anger at being forced to give up your child, the dream she would someday come back into your life. The knowledge this will never happen.

Courtney dumped the satchel out.

Her phone's light revealed the greeting cards, the newspaper clippings, and a lock of blonde hair tied with a pink ribbon. A small, silver paring knife, the blade corroded with dried blood, stuck tip first into the pile of cards. The blade taunted Courtney, an old friend whose touch she'd not felt in over a decade.

A real friend.

Something flickered in the darkness. Afraid someone might be coming, Courtney turned off the flashlight, not wishing to be discovered. The act turned out to be moot when she heard the soft mewing, and she knew the source of the flickering. She doubted a spirit cared much about flashlights.

The ghost lady, her neck bent, and her face obscured, complete with a tray in hand and gliding through the woods. Glowing in a brilliant white aura, nothing seemed to hinder the ghost's movement.

Courtney pulled up the sleeves on her sweater and flicked the flashlight back on, exposing the horizontal scar tissue crossing her forearms. One more reminder of her past.

"I'm your mother," she whispered. Tears cascaded from her eyes.

The spirit floated past headstones and Courtney, fluttering into the small chapel. She watched it pass, then she fished into her pocket to retrieve her lighter. She picked up the lock of hair, lit it on fire with one flick of her thumb, and dropped it on the cards and paper.

The knife held the paper in place as it burst into flames. She watched it flare and engulf the pile. Sixteen years of appropriated memories, immolated in a matter of seconds. It burned out, leaving behind nothing but ash, charred cardboard, and carbon-scored steel.

She pulled the knife out of the ground and slipped it into her back pocket. Courtney turned her attention to the chapel, walking to it, and stepping inside the open door.

Hanging above the threshold, hung an ancient, dry-rotting taxidermied deer head. Half its face was caved in, the one-eyed sentinel greeted parishioners with a sarcastic, toothy grin.

This didn't surprise her, nor did the ghost's aura lighting up a pew. Courtney walked down the aisle and sat on the pew next to the specter, the tray across its astral lap. She looked over, onto the tray, thinking she'd see something.

No.

And she did see something.

Please, no.

The tray's surface, scored with horizontal slashes, shimmered before her. The scars on her forearms itched in response. She wanted to cry, but couldn't. There was no more feeling left inside her. Only a friend she could rely on could help her through this. She could call on them at any time.

She turned her phone off, put it in her pocket, and sat with the spirit, basking in its ethereal light. The ghost's covered face stared at something from another life. Courtney remained in place, watching as the lunar haze of her ghostly companion flickered. The flashing hypnotized her, once again bringing her attention to her arms and the pink horizontal slashes of the scarring, hidden under the sleeves of her sweater.

The ghostly matron shimmered and faded away, disappearing from view in Courtney's peripheral vision. Now alone, in the darkness, the woman's broken soul rejoiced as an epiphany surfaced in her mind.

Courtney DeJulio knew who to call on, the one friend she could count on to help, to remedy this great malaise. The implement rested in her pocket, the one friend who never hurt her. She'd take advantage of this opportunity to become reacquainted with her long, lost friend.

And this time?

She'd try something different, and cut against the grain.

ALIVE INSIDE

I miss normality. For three years my reality has been white and sanitary, in a room roughly sixteen feet wide and 30 feet long. I still don't know what happened or why I'm here. Shit, I don't even know where *here* is. I haven't seen sunlight or another human since I woke up in this place, and I have to wonder if either still exist. In spite of the unsolved mysteries at hand, I'm alive and healthy. My captors, whomever they may be, see to it.

I follow the same routine every day. I wake up. I drone the day away. Food is delivered to me thrice daily through an automated, sealed drawer. When I go to bed, sleep eludes me at first, as I daydream of my life before all of this. When I was Jenny Roberts and my list of priorities included my family, social media, selfies and boys. These memories soon turn to nightmares.

My sister is helping Mom finish the dishes from dinner. I'm coming in from taking out the trash while the dog licks his bowl clean of beef chunk gravy and the cat nibbles away at a pile of white fish. Dad grabs the dog's leash for his obligatory after chow walk. Christine McVie and Fleetwood Mac are on the radio telling someone they make loving fun when she's interrupted in mid-sentence by the Emergency Alert klaxon.

At this moment everything changes. Throughout the house, electronic devices follow suit and a chorus of bedlam and chaos ensues in accompaniment. The dog barks as the alarm assaults his sensitive hearing, the cat hissing in fear. It's the perfect soundtrack for a disaster.

"Virginia, help your sister pack!" Mom orders me. There is no explanation, we put what little we can in shoulder bags and backpacks. Everything goes in the car. We pull out of the garage, our economy sedan now a clown car filled with humans and animals.

We're in sync with the rest of the neighborhood. The result is a slow moving line of cars inching toward the college's football stadium. Armed police and National Guard soldiers surround the school grounds when we arrive. It seems like the whole town is there.

They are.

We're directed to a parking spot and we bring ourselves and what little we can carry into the stadium. After walking through a scanner checking for Lord knows what, we are all cleared to enter, even the dog and cat. Our area is somewhere near the 35 yard line of the home team. The adrenaline subsides and one by one my family all falls asleep from exhaustion.

The nightmare isn't over, not by a long shot.

I wake up to the roar of thunder as the stadium lamps erupt, bathing everything in white light. Everyone and everything around me dead. Thousands of people, on the ground and rising up into the seats, all with horrified expressions frozen on their faces. My cat is rigid and cold in my grasp, its head missing. I drop the feline corpse and find myself curling into a fetal position in the center of it all. Before long men in yellow bio-hazard suits surround me. All I can do is sit there catatonic, staring. The last living, human face I see is through a faceplate. It's a middle-aged man, and he looks terrified.

I toss and turn, half asleep, frustrated and alone, the lucid nightmares playing on repeat until I wake up again and the cycle starts anew.

Except for today. Today is different.

It started off as usual. White lights waking me from my horrible dreams. I took a shower and all was fine until breakfast failed to arrive. This was a first, and despite the inconvenience, it was something I could live with. When lunch skipped town, I grew concerned. Was this to be my fate, to starve to death, trapped in this cell? The hours passed, the hunger pangs in my belly grew more and more intense. Irritated, I resolved not to become scared unless dinner didn't come.

To add to my stress my tablet was acting funny. As a last resort I decided to restart it. In doing so, I reset the tablet to factory presets. Much to my surprise, it found a wi-fi signal.

I feel my heart skip a beat. Without hesitation, I open

the web browser and disappointment floods my body when I get an error. The sound of a ringing phone startles me. I look, and see the Face Time app flashing, indicating an incoming call. It continues ringing, panic preventing me from answering it. I press the screen on the green icon to stop the ringing more than to answer the call.

A man's face appears on the screen. I stare in shock, not sure of what to say to the first human I've seen in three years. I can't speak. He is young and attractive, further capturing my tongue. After a silent eternity, he smiles and breaks the ice.

"Hello, Virginia, I'm Rudy. We need to talk."

"Who are you?" I reply, still shocked I'm actually speaking to a person.

"Who I am isn't important. Who *you* are, is," he pauses, his eyes looking up as he seeks the right word, "paramount." The excitement of the moment turns to anxiety. My pulse is racing, competing with my grumbling stomach for attention. I'm not very kind when I'm hungry.

"Where's my breakfast and lunch? Or better yet, how about you let me out of here? That would be a great start to my day. I'm sorry, afternoon. It's past lunch."

"I can't let you out, but I will ensure you are fed, and soon."

"You can't let me out? Of course you can't let me out. I'm stupid to even think this would be an option, ain't I. What the fuck? I've been in here three goddamn years and I don't get to know why? Prisoners in my time at least got yard time." He remained silent as I verbally bludgeoned him, "O.K., then tell me what is so fucking special about me? Why am I here? Who are you? What are you doing here?"

"Calm down, please," he turns his head, then shoots it back, "listen, I don't have much time. I understand why you are freaking out."

"Freaking out?" I interrupt him, "You haven't seen freaking out yet."

"I hope it doesn't happen, then. Listen, there was a terrorist attack on this facility."

"A terrorist attack? A fucking terrorist attack? Really? And what facility are we in that deserves the attention of terrorists?"

"I can't tell you where you are, I'm sorry," he again pauses, "some people don't agree with what we're doing here. Let's put it that way."

"What way is that? Are they pissed you're keeping an innocent woman in a hermetically sealed container like a pet?" I want food and answers, but most of all I want out of this shit hole.

"It's much more than you can understand, Virginia." His head turns, he has a worried look. I snap a screen shot of his face, "I wanted to let you know dinner was coming. I have to go. I will reach out to you tomorrow." The call ends. I stare at the tablet screen for what seems an eternity, unblinking, trying to absorb it all, not believing any of it occurred.

I open the Face Time app and look at the time stamp as proof I didn't imagine this. One call, three minutes and thirteen seconds long. I talked to a person. *A person!* A tap on the photo album reveals his screen shot. He was handsome, with steel blue eyes, a chiseled chin and dark hair. Less than five minutes of conversation with someone had happened, and I was a bitch to him. What was I thinking?

Dinner arrives. The tray is overflowing with battered, fried seafood. It's a feast of shrimp, scallops and clam strips. I've not seen this much food since first waking up in this place. I take my time devouring the contents, savoring each bite.

My belly full, I sit on my bed reflecting on the this mentally draining day, not quite sure of what to expect tomorrow. I have one answer to my questions. I'm not alone. I rest my eyes for a moment and doze off, exhausted. There are no dreams I can recall.

I'm woken by the ringing of the tablet's Face Time. Disoriented, I swipe the right button and the call connects. My eyes focus on Rudy's smile.

"Good morning, Virginia. Do you remember my name?" he asks.

"Of course I do," I reply, "Rudy," I snap another screen shot.

"Good. I trust you got your meal yesterday?"

"Yes, I did. You outdid yourself."

"I thought you'd like that. A fed Virginia is easier to talk to, I see."

"Of course she is," I try to hide my smile but I think I fail. Perhaps he's right. I decide to be more open and casual.

"Breakfast is on its way," he continued, returning my smirk with one of his own, "I don't expect us to have another incident."

"You said it was a terrorist attack?"

"Yes," he replies with hesitation, "you could say that."

"I didn't," I remind him, "you did."

"Yes, I did. It's complicated, Virginia."

"You can call me Jenny, it's what my friends call me," I tell him, "if you are my friend."

"I'm your friend, Jenny, yes," he sighs and looks off camera, at what I cannot see.

"Then why am I in here?" I demand, "Tell me." I look him in the eye. He doesn't answer fast enough. "Tell me, goddammit. Tell me what happened!"

"I don't know where to begin," he looks empathetic, or he fakes it well, "Shit, I don't know where I can begin."

"We could start with who put me here. How about that?"

"*Them.* You know, the figurative *They* who run everything," he shook his head in disapproval, "this has all been *Their* doing."

"But why?"

"You are the key to unlocking a mystery, Jenny."

"How so?" I feel irritation rising in my belly and spreading through my body like the noise of an ambulance siren as it gets closer to you, "I'm sure you can tell me why I'm so special I have to be locked in a bunker."

"I can't."

"Why not?" I push the issue.

"Because. I can't." His tone becomes frustrated. I decide to escalate things and say fuck it all to being well fed and nicer.

"No? O.K., then. I don't think we need to talk." I hang up the call.

I wait an hour for Rudy to call back. He doesn't. I try calling him. The tablet rings but he doesn't answer. Breakfast comes, I push it aside. I don't want food, I want answers and I'm not getting them eating. Frustrated, I bury my face in the pillows of my bed.

I've still got half a plate of cold pancakes and sausage when lunch arrives, a cheese steak with whiz and chocolate milkshake. I grab the milkshake, wrap the blankets around me and come to a decision as I suck the delicious treat through the straw. I'm not getting up today except to eat and use the toilet. Not until I get answers. I sit in silence staring at my bunk and the tablet until the lights shut down.

I'm unable to sleep, my mind now obsessing on Rudy and my mistake. After some hours of this, I start wishing for sleep and the nightmares. Anything could be better than this emptiness. I once read in some book hell isn't a place, it's a feeling, an emptiness caused by being separated from God. I think I can relate after being detached from human contact, then having a taste of it, only for it to be removed. This is surely is hell.

A narrow beam of light shines through the observation window, catching me by surprise. I see a person standing on the other side of the window. It's a man, about six feet in height, wearing a biohazard suit. I can hardly see his face under the hood of the protective screen, but I know who it is, there's no one else it could be. Rudy looks straight at me, our eyes connect. Something instinctual stirs in my body. I place my hand on the plexiglass, he does the same, only there's a dry erase board with words on it in his hand.

I CAN'T TALK TO YOU ON A DEVICE. SOMEONE WILL FIND OUT. I'LL BE REMOVED FROM THE PROJECT.

"What project?" I say out loud. He erases his last statement and scribbles down a few words.

DON'T SPEAK, THEY CAN HEAR YOU! He looks scared. He writes down a considerable amount of words. THREE YEARS AGO THE ZIKA VIRUS MUTATED, DRIVING INFECTED PEOPLE TO VIOLENCE. THEY WENT ON KILLING SPREES.

I stare at the words in disbelief. He's telling me there has been...

A REAL ZOMBIE APOCALYPSE. GOVERNMENTS FELL, MILLIONS DIED. He pulls the board back, erasing then writing more. YOU ARE THE ONLY HUMAN BEING EXPOSED TO THE VIRUS WHO'S LIVED.

Oh, my God. It's the end of the world and I'm trapped in a bunker, a prisoner of the last remaining human population? The Walking Dead wasn't a fantasy for emo kids, bored housewives and their workaholic husbands? I thought back to the football stadium. It all started to make sense. He writes more.

THE PEOPLE WHO BROUGHT YOU HERE FELL TO THE VIRUS. THE ACTING GOVERNMENT KEPT YOU QUARANTINED HERE. YOUR DNA MATERIAL HAS BEEN TESTED FOR ANTIBODIES TO PROTECT THE REST OF THE POPULATION FROM THE BUG.

I realize I don't have any writing implements, so I improvise and use the tablet's text screen. I type a question and press the table to the window.

I'M SORRY I HUNG UP ON YOU.

He scribbles down a reply. IT'S OK. I HAVE TO BE CAREFUL, NO ONE KNOWS WE ARE TALKING. NO ONE CAN EVER KNOW.

WHY ALL THE SECRETS?

NOT EVERYONE IS HAPPY YOU ARE HERE.

WHY? I push the issue.

WE BELIEVE YOU'RE THE CURE.

THE CURE?

YES.

I DON'T UNDERSTAND. IF I AM THE CURE, THEN WHY ALL OF THIS? I plead.

I'M SORRY, I CAN'T TELL YOU ANYMORE. He appears concerned.

PLEASE? I beg.

I'VE BEEN GONE TOO LONG. I'LL SLIP YOU MORE WHEN I CAN. HAVE TO GO. Before I can reply, he wipes the board off and walks away.

Within moments the only light comes from my tablet. I fall back onto my bed and wrap myself in the blankets.

Rudy's picture stares at me from the tablet. For the first time in a long time I don't feel like a prisoner. Sleep comes and with it clarified memories, much to my horror.

From our home to the stadium, my brain is on fast forward, speeding through the commercials of a DVR recording, then it slows to real time. We're sitting at the thirty-five yard line, me, my Mom, Dad, my sister, the dog and cat. We're surrounded by thousands of people, all of them families, like ours. The low buzz of people whispering in fear to one another permeates the air, transforming into a roar of panic. It fills the stadium, spreading in a chain reaction, masses of persons all around the edges of the stadium are snapping up in twisted, unnatural postures. This launches a domino effect spreading inward toward the field. People scream in fear as their neighbors turn and attack them, arms flailing in the air, striking at anyone and everyone nearby. Mouths snap their jaws, biting and attacking anything within reach. With no place else to run, everyone stays in place, they can only wait for the ripples of violence spreading through the masses to reach them.

My mother hugs my father, my sister grasps our mother with one arm and the dog with the other. I hold the cat and press as close into our father's side as I can. We're all shaking in fear. We are not alone, nor is our terror unjustified. Our dog breaks free of my sister's grasp and pounces on a man charging toward our general direction. Fido's jaws sink into the man's neck, ripping his throat out before he reaches us. The dog shakes his head. Blood and pieces of flesh fly about, covering those nearby in gore. A crazed woman attacks the family next to us, tearing into them with fists flying and teeth gnashing. The blood shower catches their attention. The woman and those around her, raging like lunatics, all fall onto Fido. He has no chance, they're faster. The barking is replaced by a muffled squeal and the sounds of bones cracking.

I feel a tug on my lap. It's Snuffy, his claws digging into my legs. I reach down to calm my cat and feel a wetness on my finger tips. I look at my hand, it's covered in blood, and I'm shocked to find Snuffy has been beheaded. I hear a crunching noise to my left, it's coming from my sister, a twisted grimace adorns her face. She's chewing on a mouthful of *Lordknowswhat*. She sticks her tongue out at me, I see hair the color of Snuffy's caught in her teeth and a familiar feline eyeball rolling on her tongue. Cranial fluid drips from the corner of her lip.

"What did you do?" I scream and push her away. She's holding Snuffy's head in her hand, now a calico patterned apple with a chunk bitten out of it. Blood splashes on my face from above. I look up and find my mother has sunk her teeth into my father's neck, ripping his throat open. Dad falls to the ground and his head bounces off the turf. Mom stands, gore dripping off her face, she looks to me and smiles. My mother rears her head back to strike, all I can do is scream and piss myself.

The blow never comes. Instead, she collapses into a pile behind me. My sister does the same, her mouth lolling open, bits of cat falling out of it. It doesn't stop there. The people next to us, the people next to them, the crazy people and the victims, all them start falling to the ground, one by one. Within minutes I'm surrounded by tens of thousands of dead people. I'm too terrified to scream.

The tablet wakes me up, buzzing and ringing in the dark. I fumble for the tablet and see the screen. It's Rudy! My heart pounds my chest like a clenched fist. I answer the call and his face comes on the screen.

"Hello!" I say, excited.

"Hi, Jenny," he replies, "You're awful perky for a girl who just learned she's in a survivor's enclave after a zombie apocalypse."

"You know how it is, it's all about the company you keep," I wink at him. He doesn't seem to notice.

"I've got great news for you. We think there has been a breakthrough in the clinicals."

"Clinicals?"

"Yes, you know, the tests for a cure."

"Oh?" I wonder what he's trying to get at, but I can't help but stare at his deep, blue eyes.

"Today you're going to get a visitor," he replies. This catches my attention.

"Oh, really?"

"Really." He's sporting a big toothy grin, "OK, I have to go. Just try to look surprised in ten minutes when your breakfast arrives."

"O.K." I reply. He's still smiling when the call goes dark. What could he be talking about? Is this going to be an extra special breakfast? Maybe some gourmet omelet? For ten long minutes I sit in waiting.

After not seeing or hearing or touching another person in ages, I can assume it's only natural I would become infatuated with Rudy. After all, he appeared to be near me in age. I would gaze at his picture, fantasizing about being out of this prison, in his arms, without a biohazard suit on or plexiglass separating us. What would we say to one another? What would we do? What could we do?

Each fantasy leads to more questions, pulling me deeper into the illusion. What are his interests? Does he have a family? What is his job here? I feel a stirring in my belly, an almost nauseous disorientation of my insides. It's a carnal feeling, making me shake with anticipation thinking about it. Butterflies were sinking deep into my abdomen, their wings fluttering and tickling every exposed nerve inside me.

I decide to take a shower, thinking it will clear my mind, but it only exacerbates the feelings. The water is relaxing, tingling my soul as it bounces and rolls off my skin. I close my eyes. Hormones flow through my body, making me shiver despite the heat of the water. He's still on my mind as I turn off the spigot, open the door and step out onto the cold concrete floor. A chill runs up my spine. I jump back into bed as the lights shut off, curling up in my blankets. My long hair is dripping wet, but I don't care. Each drop on my shoulder or back is a reminder of Rudy.

The buzzer sounds and I hear the serving window open. I see it's a tray of breakfast goodies, as predicted. I snatch it up and carry it back to my table, wondering what's so special about it. I see eggs, bacon, hash browns and toast, with orange juice to wash it down. A typical breakfast with nothing out of the ordinary to it.

The buzzer rings again, the air replies, and the window opens. An orange tabby kitten hops out. It runs to my feet and starts to roll about on the floor in front of me. I reach down and pick it up, careful of its claws and teeth. The little cat has a collar, and a name tag. "CAT 09," it reads.

A few minutes later, the buzzer goes off again, this time ushering in a cat box, litter and cans of cat food. There is a note, it looks to be in Rudy's handwriting.

It's not up to me to name this animal, she's been vaccinated with anti-bodies created from your blood. If nothing is abnormal, it's only a matter of time before you can be released. I won't be in touch for a couple days. Rudy.

The kitten resembles Snuffy, my cat from before. "That's your name, little bit, Snuffy. Yes, I'll call you Snuffy," I scratch kitty's wee head. She purrs in response, rubbing her head into my palm.

Snuffy follows me about as I work out and get my daily exercise. There's begging when lunch and dinner come, which I gladly enable. Fur, razor-sharp claws, needle-pointed teeth and a sandpaper tongue are my delights of the day.

I pick up my tablet to play some music, and notice I have an email alert. I open the app and see an unopened email, the sender's address is blank, as is the subject line. Inside there is a series of URLs and nothing else. No signature, nothing to indicate what the URLs are for. I click on one of the links, the browser opens and takes me to a video.

I launch what I assume to be a movie, but it's a news report produced after the outbreak, theorizing how the bodies of those who should be dead still walked. The talking heads believed the Zika virus had bonded with the HIV virus, allowing the new super-virus to high-jack the victim's DNA and genetic code with unforeseen results.

All living things have a genetic off switch, according to the taking heads. When a person suffers from a fall or a gun shot, the damage done by the condition may or may not trigger a chemical response saying *This can't be fixed.* The order is then given on a genetic level to shut things down. Muscles, nerves and electrical pulses cease to operate on command ushering in dirt nap time with zero chance of recovery.

The mutated virus disabled this self-destruct mechanism. People with mortal wounds lived regardless of missing limbs or other maladies. Their brains, damaged by encephalitis, turned the infected bestial and violent, giving unlife to the stereotypical zombie of Hollywood lore.

I absorb all of it, but part of me can't help but wonder. Why had none of the stories mentioned me, the famous cure for the disease? If I'm so integral to all of this, why am I not in any of the material? Lights out comes. Snuffy snuggles up in the crook of arm, purring away and sending me into a deep, dreamless sleep.

I'm shaken awake by a roar of thunder. Snuffy is still tucked under my arm, the kitten unimpressed by the echoing boom. *What is it? Another terrorist attack,* I wonder? I feel for the cat and pat her side. Snuffy turns her head to me, opens her eyes and yawns.

"Stay here," I tell Snuffy, and hop off the bunk. The floor is cold, curling my toes on contact. Another loud boom sounds through my dormitory, shaking the walls. This can't be good. I search for my tablet to reach out to Rudy and find out what is going on. I find it tangled in the blankets on my bed. I open its case, the screen's light illuminates the room, but I find there is no wi-fi signal.

"Dammit!" I shout in frustration. I toss the tablet back on my bunk and pace about the cell, absently chewing on my hair, trying not to be scared but I'm terrified. I see dust falling from above in the light from my tablet. The kitten jumps off the bunk and comes to my side. I reach down and pick Snuffy up, hugging her close to my chest. She's purring, the poor thing is too young to know fear.

I almost drop the cat when Rudy appears on the other side of the window. He's not wearing a biohazard suit. He's in jeans, a hoodie and sneakers, not an alien hiding behind rubber and plastic from an unknown horror. He says something I can't hear because of the glass, but he's waving his arms for me to back away. Rudy pulls up a shotgun and empties six rounds in a semi-circle into the plexiglass. It shatters, pressurized air rushes out of my dorm, a now scared Snuffy is hissing in unison.

"I knew the antigen worked! Cat Oh Nine!" he screams in victory, thrusting his arm holding the shotgun into the air.

"I named her Snuffy," I tell him as he steps through the broken frame, into my dormitory.

"I knew it! I knew we had to have it, otherwise they wouldn't have attacked, again."

"Who?" I ask.

"The terrorists? Rebels who didn't think we could protect us from you."

"Protect you from," I pause, unsure of the word to use. It falls off my lips, "me?" He sits on my bunk and beckons me to join him.

"Sit down, please," he pats the bed. I join him, placing my knee so it touches his, sending a shiver up my spine, "you are the only person who didn't succumb to the virus, but it's in your body, locked in a previous state. Your presence turns back on the genetic coding the virus's mutation shut off. The other doctors think it has something to do with your pheromones. As a result, you are deadly to the infected."

"And who is that?" I ask.

"Every other warm blooded, living thing on this planet," he replied. My gift was a cat who may have lived or died because of her association with me and the disease I carry but am immune to. I'm a regular Typhoid Mary. He puts his hand on my knee, bringing the butterflies back to my belly. This is really happening.

"So why can you be around me?" I ask him, "aren't you infected?"

"I was, but I'm still alive for the same reason Cat Oh Nine, I mean Snuffy, is. I took the antigen, stole it from the doctors and injected it into myself. See? I'm fine."

I don't waste another moment. I grab his face and pull it to mine, locking my lips to his in a deep kiss. He doesn't resist. We are both shaking in a combination of fear and excitement. I work at unbuttoning his jeans as he takes his shirt off. He pushes me back onto the bed and draws himself forward on top of me. My sexual experiences before this were limited to heavy petting and hand jobs. I let him control me, guide me, the cotton between our sexes barely preventing the inevitable coitus. I reach down and free him from the restraints of his boxers, it's larger than I imagined. I reposition my ass, allowing him easier access to enter me. He slips on a condom before mounting me.

"You don't mind, do you?" He asks me, an embarrassed, boyish grin on his face.

"Just fuck me, please." With a free hand I guide him. He pushes forward, my hymen resisting at first, then it gives way with a slight sting. The pain is soon offset by pleasure, stimulating every nerve ending in my body. He builds up a rhythm, rocking back and forth, in and out of me. I'm in bliss, I never want this to end, but it does.

I feel a pinch, something sharp is sticking into my back, taking me out of the moment. Rudy has his eyes closed, still lost in ecstasy. His thrusting has numbed me to the point where I can't feel him, though I know he's still inside me. I reach an arm behind me and find a wetness on the bed where there shouldn't be any.

What the hell? I feel about and discover what is stabbing me, a piece of metal. I pull it out from under me and see "CAT 09" written on the tag. Bits of bone and fur mixed with slimy goo are dripping off it. I Look up to Rudy and open my mouth to scream. He moans and opens his eyes.

Rudy's eyeballs fall out of his face into my mouth in unison. The optic nerves, stretched thin, snap as they pop out. One slides down my throat, triggering my gag reflex, and I spit them both out. As a reaction I push Rudy back off me. He flops to the side, twisting a leg backwards. His penis, still inside me, snaps off at the base. I yank it out by the condom and remaining flesh, the latex inclosed dead member popping from the suction. It melts in my hand, dripping out of the flaccid rubber.

Rudy is starting to rot on the bed next to me. His flesh is a melting candle, liquefying and exposing bone and tissue. His chest caves in, his eyeless face collapses. Within moments he's a puddle of goo. I jump off the bed, slipping on the floor, moving as far away from what used to be Rudy and Snuffy as I can.

I grab my clothes and get dressed. I'm about to leave the dorm when a trio of men in biohazard suits appear in the observation bay. They look terrified. After what I experienced, they should be.

"Ms. Roberts," the lead man says, "please, remain in your dormitory. We can't allow you to leave."

"And what happens if I do?" I make a threatening move toward him. He shirks back.

"Your blood is dangerous. That foolish Rudy didn't

listen. Please, please, I plead with you, stay in the cell. We're here to protect you," I dub him Mr. Talks Too Much.

"No, you aren't. You're here to keep me a prisoner. And I'm not going to do it anymore!" I rush at them. One trips and takes out his buddy. Now known as Dipsy Dumb and Dipsy Dumber, they both face plant next to Mr. Talks Too Much. Dumber's face plate has cracked. He starts screaming, pushing his body away from me. It doesn't matter. I watch his face melt as his body slumps and crumbles inside the suit.

"Please, Ms. Roberts! Don't do this! We've kept you alive!"

"No, you've kept me a prisoner!" I punch him in the face. The hood of the biohazard suit rips. He tries saying something but his lips and throat rot away before he's able. In seconds he's starting to decay into goo. The last guy is crying, begging me for mercy. What mercy do I have to give other than a swift death? I rip open his suit and place my hand on his breast. His chest implodes on contact; black, rotting organs pop and spew gray and green slime on the floor before turning to dust.

They left the door open in their haste to contain me. I walk into the deserted facility, fire alarms ringing and echoing throughout. Emergency lights spray their jaundiced glow, guiding me away from my containment unit, past laboratories and animal testing cages. My path comes to one last door, the exit out. I open it and step outside.

The sun embraces me for the first time in years,

warming my exposed skin. I take my first deep breath of freedom. Smoke billows from the roof of the facility, where the terrorist's bombs went off. The building is surrounded by thousands of people, half of them protesting my right to exist, the other half standing up for my rights as a human being. The only thing they share is the virus.

I take another step forward, the breeze caressing my hair, lifeless bodies falling to the ground at my feet with each step forward. I see a trio of guards dropping their guns and running away from me as fast as undead muscles can propel them. It's too late. I'm learning my presence triggers their repressed genetics, and long dead bodies held together by broken DNA find themselves rotting on the concrete.

I'm a walking plague. The masses gathered at the gates of the facility have no options other than to die as I stroll by the fence. It's a chain reaction of decaying dominoes, spreading out from where I stand. I reach the main gates of the compound. The mob of protestors parts, to give me a clear path. The poor bastards don't even have time to scream, their DNA is jump started before their synapses can fire. They die by the hundreds, by the thousands, in only seconds.

I think about Rudy one last time, still tasting his kiss and feeling his embrace. I won't be haunted by his death, in fact, it only motivates me to carry on. I doubt I'll ever find another person like me, immune to the infection. It doesn't matter, without Rudy, I don't want anyone else. I'm destined to be alone for the remainder of my days.

PART TWO
...PEOPLE ARE.

THE HATE-BOX IN HER HEART

Before anyone could stop her, the dog ate the shit out of Randy Wilson's soiled blue jeans. Big, dumb, and blonde, Cheyenne the Golden Retriever was in her glory. She dug in, pulling the dungarees away, all while licking the greasy excrement up like it was peanut butter. The feces resembled wet clay and smelled like week old sauerkraut left on the counter. The dog's snout was covered in fecal matter, slicked back and off-color as a result. It looked as if she assisted Demi Moore and Patrick Swayze at the potter's wheel.

Randy found himself in a predicament, kneeling at the porcelain altar after drinking his face off at their annual Memorial Day party. He made it to the bathroom, a miracle in and of itself. It was a small victory in a war he was destined to lose. While kneeling and regurgitating the alcohol in his belly, his bowels let loose.

He shit himself like a champ.

He screamed and fell to his side on the bathroom

faux-tile flooring. He unbuttoned his pants, kicking and squirming out of them. He hoped what felt like a cable of turd remained mostly intact. It did. It resembled a milk chocolate hot dog, much to Cheyenne's joy and Sarah Wilson's disgust. The dog gobbled the fecal treat up with glee. The woman was of another opinion.

Randy's wife stood in the bathroom door, looking at him, shaking her head, not knowing what to do. This wasn't the first time he'd gotten hammered. In any other circumstance, it wouldn't have been a problem. But tonight, with the company they brought into their house, he should have known better. Not like he really cared about it right now. Randy was naked as a newborn baby and just as vulnerable. Loud snoring indicated Randy had passed out on the linoleum flooring. Then Sarah remembered she wasn't alone.

Every living soul from the party was watching this happen. Randy didn't bother closing the door to the bathroom. And Sarah endured the embarrassment of it all in front of the party goers. She loved her husband, but tonight was a bit too much. He binge drank without eating beforehand, and now they both paid for his poor judgment.

It burned a hole in Sarah's ass, knowing she made a spread of food more for her husband than for the people there. It was all his favorites. Could Randy be bothered to eat any of it? No. She spent all day preparing baked ziti, macaroni and cheese, seven layer taco dip, and the mud pudding. Not to mention wrapping those goddamn little weenies in croissant dough. All foods Randy loved but didn't touch. Did he even understand what she went through to get the pasta the right consistency for serving?

What a fucking retard, Sarah thought, *he doesn't even know what al dente means.* The dog ran past her, nearly knocking Sarah on her ass. Randy's shit ridden boxers were held fast in Cheyenne's bite. Sarah stepped back to avoid the dog's bulk and tripped over Randy's sneakers. She caught herself from falling by grabbing the shower curtain. A few ringlets popped out and ricocheted through the standing bath. The curtain ripped and would need to be replaced. One more bit of unluck to pile on her stack of bullshit tonight.

She lost her composure.

"Everyone out of the fucking house!" Sarah screamed, "go back to the garage, out by the pool, anywhere but here until I get this motherfucking mess cleaned up!" She threw Randy's sneakers out of the bathroom. They clunked off the wall in synchronized thuds. The house cleared out of guests. No one asked if she needed help. They all knew better.

Sarah Wilson was a good person. At least, she believed herself to be. Anyone who met her would have said she was nice, maybe a little difficult to work with, but at least she was polite about it. Sarah's O.C.D. made her want to excel at whatever she was part of. If she couldn't ace it, she could always burn it and make it go away. And if something rubbed her fucking wrong, well, it could burn too. A decade working at a footwear factory in Indiana made her hate shoes. Her disdain was so severe, she wore flip flops whenever possible. This wasn't always the case.

There was a time when Sarah loved shoes. Back when she first met Randy at the plant in Fenton, New York.

The Fenton Catheter plant was a shitty place to work. Sarah Pluff met Randy Wilson there, and they fell in love. But the plant had a strict no fraternization policy, especially between supervisors and those working under them. Randy was Sarah's boss. But they fell in love anyway and kept it from the powers that be for three years before anyone got wind of it.

A salesman wooing new clients from a Japanese hospital chanced upon them at their secret getaway, a karaoke bar in Fenton called Rafferty's. Sarah and Randy chose this place because no one who worked at the plant would ever be caught dead in a karaoke bar. Now the cat was out of the bag. The Monday after, the two of them were brought into Human Resources. Randy was fired on the spot, and Sarah was put on probation.

This was okay with Randy. He and Sarah were now able to get on with their lives together. Randy's on the job experience got him a similar position at a bottler in nearby Fulton. Soon after, the two married and all was well. Sarah, on the other hand, wasn't happy about it at all. She stewed on it for years to follow. Sarah looked for an excuse to even the score with the management at the plant. She never got the chance. Ten years ago, when the bottler in Fulton closed and the Fenton Catheter plant burned to the ground, she finally found it. The local news called it a tragic turn of events in an already economically depressed city.

Randy and Sarah had packed up and moved here from northern New York. It was a dream job. The Harrison Shoe

Factory allowed them both to work, albeit on different shifts. Of course, the economy was better then. But as we all know, nothing good lasts forever. Soon the area they lived in grew more and more poverty-stricken, with foreclosures and brownfields. The last couple of years were the worst. Morale in the plant was at an all-time low. They cut vacation time and overtime first. Then the rumors of the plant shutting down and moving to China or, worse, Canada, started circulating.

Yes, Sarah cultivated a special place in the *hate-box* of her heart for footwear, shoes and sneakers in particular. It was tucked away in a corner and tied up with a pretty little bow, next to a pair of ex-boyfriends and the catheter manufacturing plant. All three smoldered in her memories like the cherry cores of charcoal briquettes, shimmering with heat, wisping away the smoke of the fires from long ago.

The oven beeped, signaling the fresh pan of baked ziti was done warming up. Sarah was a master of the baked ziti. Family members and co-workers over the years always called her when they needed a ziti for an event. Graduations, church functions, baby showers, or funerals. The latter being the most popular. So popular, in fact, Sarah's ziti came to be known as the *Death Ziti* in some circles. Did somebody die? Call Sarah, she'll bake a killer ziti for the reception.

Sarah remembered the baked zitis at receptions she'd gone to in the past were always bad. Like her boyfriend in high school, Jeremy. The ziti at his funeral sucked.

Back when Sarah wasn't Sarah Wilson, when she was Sarah

Pluff, a teenager growing up in Fenton, NY, she went to the Junior prom with her boyfriend, Jeremy Simmons. After the formalities and a bottle of menthol schnapps, Jeremy thought drunk Sarah and he should consummate the night without her permission. He felt she had held back long enough after going steady for the whole school year, and needed some coaxing. If you asked him about it in the limited number of days he had left to follow, he'd say it was good for him.

A week later, Sarah didn't resist when he didn't ask for permission again. Jeremy took her to a secret camping spot. She let him violate her to validate her hate for this boy. The girl was peeing behind a tree, crying as he dripped out of her. She felt herself drift off, but when the sleeping bag burst into flames, all she could do was watch it consume Jeremy.

Sarah was lucky, they said. The sleeping bag was too close to their campfire. It was a tragic accident, people said. At the reception, they consoled his family, and even Sarah, for those who knew the pair were in a relationship.

She used the excuse of the mourners and their condolences as a reason not to eat the shitty baked ziti. It was dry, with an awful aftertaste, and the top was burned. She could still see the black tips of the pasta poking out of the browned cheese. They reminded her of Jeremy's charcoaled fingers and toes poking through the burnt nylon fabric of the sleeping bag.

"Fuck!" Reality brought back the present. Sarah stood in the hallway between the bathroom and the kitchen, her mind twisting as she triaged the situation. Randy was passed out on the floor, he could wait. She couldn't see the dog anywhere, but the stench of smeared shit permeated the house. The hound was nearby, no doubt. The ziti, however, was going to burn, and she couldn't have that. Sarah dashed to the stove, grabbed the oven mitts, and removed it from the oven. The foil tray bowed from the weight of holding three pounds of pasta, ground beef, spaghetti sauce, and mozzarella. Steam rose from the dish, and for a brief moment, the sulphuric stink of crap was covered by the aroma of a freshly baked ziti.

Sarah set the potholders aside. Looking out the window, she saw the partygoers were still milling about the garage, drinking, listening to music. This was a good thing. This gave her time to tend to her husband, get him out of the bathroom and into their bed. He remained unconscious, laying on the floor naked. All she had to do was wake him up and she could get the ziti out to the party and enjoy herself. Cheyenne stood at the door in the kitchen, her face no longer noticeably shit slicked. The dog cleaned up well. Sarah opened the door and let the animal run out.

"Randy, get up. Come on. You've got to get out of this room." Sarah slapped his face, taking some frustration out on him in the process. This meant she hit him harder than needed. All she got for a response was a soft gurgling moan. She sat him up. His body was limp and inert, and he crumbled back onto the floor, prone. Sarah swore softly under her breath. This wasn't working. His skin was cold and clammy, not to mention the white pallor covering his body.

Sarah sat on the floor next to her husband, frustrated

and dejected. She couldn't get him to wake. His breath was soft and shallow, and sweat continued to bead across his person. She patted him down with towels. Shit was smeared everywhere, and he didn't quite get all the vomit into the toilet.

Using darker towels from the linen closet as impromptu mops, she wiped up the mess on the floor of the bathroom. The feat was accomplished in record time, less than ten minutes. Soaked towels, moist with bile and sweat, went into the hamper. She topped it off with the remaining clothes Randy left behind, amounting to a t-shirt and shit-stained jeans.

Then she remembered the ziti.

It's getting cold! "Shit!" Sarah stood straight up and ran back to the kitchen, her flip flops slapping between the sole of her foot and the floor as she went. "Fuck, fuck, fuck." She opened the oven door, picked it up with the quilted mitts and slid the tray of food back in to keep warm. She couldn't serve cold ziti. No way.

What about Randy? "Son of a bitch! Now was not the time for this!" She wasn't letting him ruin her party any further tonight. Sarah knew she needed to get him into bed, opening the bathroom back up for anyone else who might need it. She grabbed him by the arms. *Damn he really is cold*, she noted to herself, then, *At least the ziti was warm.* It was easier than she presumed to drag him from the bathroom into their nearby bedroom. He was already thin and light enough. Puking as much as he had probably shaved off another couple pounds. Sarah rolled

Randy's body onto their bed. She'd deal with this after everyone left.

Sarah Wilson was satisfied all was now under control.

She opened the oven and a blast of heat hit her in the face. It was a furnace, blurring her vision and stealing her breath. Like the heat from the club in Syracuse when she was in college.

She met the man of her dreams: Shane Parry, a long-haired rock and roller who made her forget about Jeremy's crimes. She opened up to Shane, gave him all of her, and he took this trust to the emotional bank. Shane wasn't quite a good enough singer to be in any band, but he went to the shows anyway. Sarah was his trophy girl, hanging off Shane's shoulder at the rock clubs between Buffalo and Albany whenever a good band came through the region within a five hour drive.

Shane would often disappear into the bathroom or outside the club for long periods of time. It didn't take a brain surgeon to understand he was selling drugs. This didn't bother Sarah, she could entertain herself, listening to the bands or having her own mindless conversation with one of the other abandoned girlfriends in her proximity. What bothered her was going into the green room at Mac's Bad Art Bar in Syracuse. There, she happened upon some whore snorting a line off Shane's dick. This was shocking, yes, but when the slut proceeded to blow him for the happy ending, Sarah couldn't watch. He didn't see his girlfriend, and her discovery didn't pan out as they do in porn or letters in Hustler. No, Sarah was quiet as she lit a smoke. After a couple puffs, she threw it on the floor and went outside to cry.

The reports later said a smoldering cigarette started the fire. It spread with lightning speed, cutting the green room off from any exits. A half dozen people died in the blaze, including Shane Parry and a young woman whose name has been lost to Sarah, though they mentioned it a few times on the news. If you asked Sarah, she would weep and say it was tragic.

The benefit for the club survivors served baked ziti, alongside trays of meatballs and Italian sausage, Sarah recalled. The caterer broke two cardinal rules. They didn't bake the meat with the pasta. Oh, and the sauces were different, one sweet, the other a little bitter. A huge no no. You had to put the meat in the same sauce with the pasta, you fucking idiots.

Sarah put on her best happy face and opened the door. Cheyenne slinked past her, coming back inside. The dog surprised her, and Sarah almost dropped the hot tray of food. She shot the animal a dirty look, then returned to the party with the fresh pan of ziti.

The pasta dish was a hit; Sarah knew it would be. All the food she spread out was gobbled up by her co-workers and friends.

Were they whispering about Randy while they stood at the tables grazing?

Their co-workers working the first shift the next day

left earlier, but the party didn't slow down until the wee hours of the morning.

The laughing, the giggling, was it all about Randy and their shit eating dog?

The last guest, who happened to be their neighbors traveling on foot, finally left.

They'll gossip on their way, why wouldn't they?

Sarah went back into her house. It was time for bed.

Would she be able to sleep, considering the circumstances?

The garage could be picked up and cleaned tomorrow. It was too goddamn late to play housekeeper Hazel. She took a shower to cool down. Standing in it with her hands braced on the wall, she stared at the torn curtain, running the night's events through her brain. She could smell the sick sweet stink rising from the hamper. Randy's accident earlier in the night wasn't going down without a fight. She shook her head, exhausted from it all. Sarah made a note to take care of that in the morning.

No. Wait. She corrected herself. *Randy can take care of the mess.* She did enough cleaning him up and getting him into bed.

Sarah went back to the bedroom to tend to Randy and go to bed herself. She stopped in mid-step and threw her hand over her face. Their dog was up on the bed. Randy was laying on his left side in a 'V', his butt pointed at Sarah's side of their bed. This wasn't unfamiliar territory. Cheyenne often slept with them on the bed. The dog also tended to snuggle with Randy. But this was different. Cheyenne's haunches were raised and her head was down. The dog's shoulder blades were too close to his leg. She peered over Randy's side.

Cheyenne's snout was buried up to her ears in Randy's ass crack.

"Cheyenne! No!" she screamed at the dog.

The animal ignored Sarah, it was too busy sodomizing Randy with its face. Cheyenne dug in, twisting and turning her head about within his rear end. Sarah could hear wet lapping and chewing sounds. A slow, steady drip of something came from somewhere. It made her stomach sour. One of his sneakers was by her foot; Sarah grabbed it and threw it at Cheyenne.

"I said no!" The shoe bounced off her backside, catching her attention. The dog whined and pulled back. "Oh my fucking God!"

The dog's blonde face was red and slicked back. Something fleshy and limp hung in the retriever's mouth. Sarah felt the bile rising in her throat.

"Get the fuck out of there!" she screamed again at the dog and charged in, her feet pounding on the flooring of the house.

Cheyenne bolted, dripping blood and drool from her lips onto the carpeting.

Sarah reached down and shook him. "Randy, wake up, wake the fuck up. This is enough."

He didn't respond. She turned him over.

She saw far more than she could ever imagine in the brief seconds before her face dropped into the wastebasket at their bedside. The container was quickly filled with vomit. Sarah saw what Cheyenne did to Randy's ass. Something in his shit tasted so good to the dog, she came back for a second helping. She must have licked him clean and wanted more. This is all Sarah could think of to justify the dog digging into Randy's asshole.

Like Jeremy's burned and blistered face, with the bits of nylon melted into his eyes.

Sarah now knew the identity of the mystery item Cheyenne held in her jowls.

Too bad it wasn't Shane or Jeremy's dick, she mused in her head.

A pool of black liquid, once hidden under him, now surrounded Randy on the bed, it was soaked into the mattress and dripped onto the floor below it. Sarah knelt next to it, avoiding touching the brackish pool of Randy's blood. She hurled more, her body dry heaving and convulsing, trying to get everything out of her system. Bile and bits of taco dip dripped from her lips. She wiped her mouth with a blanket, then Sarah stuffed it into the void of Randy's ass. This was less to stop the oozing of internal juices and more so she didn't have to look at the wound. She held back the tears of grief. She loved Randy, but the crying could come after she got the work done.

The night's events were more than she could take on an emotional level. The hate-box in her heart was getting filled to the brim. She was going to be a busy woman in the next twenty-four hours. She detested embarrassment. Half the people here worked in the plant with her. Embarrassment equaled failure in the eyes of the law, as far as she was concerned, and Sarah couldn't have that. Tonight, she mentally added her dead husband to the waiting list for the darkest parts of her heart, alongside the employees of Harrison Shoes, Inc. It was time for a change, again, she knew this much. She must rise from the ashes without the baggage of the world before. Sarah would need to purge once again, like she did with Jeremy, Shane, and fucking Fenton Catheter. They all made their way into the hate-box in Sarah's heart.

Tragic? Yes. Funny, Sarah thought, *no, ironic.* It was ironic how Randy's act of overdrinking and its results set this off. She knew what she needed to do. It was time for a change. Sarah Wilson turned on all the burners on the gas stove.

Maybe, just maybe, Sarah dropped Jeremy's sleeping bag onto the fire after knocking him the fuck out?

The dull, woozy non-smell of natural gas filled the kitchen and the rest of the house. Cheyenne was scratching at the door again. Sarah opened it and let the animal run off. She followed the dog outside, stepping into the driveway, watching and waiting as the house filled with the gas. Once she was satisfied the place was a gas trap, Sarah went into the garage.

Or maybe, the night she caught Shane getting his knob slobbed, Sarah dropped her cigarette on a pile of papers? Was this after locking the door to the green room? Shit, no one ever asked if she was backstage nor did she bother to offer any details.

It was still a mess from the Memorial Day party, but she retrieved an empty beer bottle from a trash bin to serve her purpose. On the floor behind a bench was a container of gasoline. The woman filled the bottle and stuffed some paper in the mouth, trapping the gas. Sarah inspected her handiwork and smiled. She went back to the driveway, took the can of gasoline, put it in the backseat of her car, and got in the vehicle.

How about ten years ago at Fenton Catheter? Sarah could have said something—done anything—about the fraying, sparking wires on a machine. She could have moved the flammable chemicals in the machine's vicinity before she left work on a Friday. She could have told a supervisor. But she didn't. Once you made it into Sarah's hate-box, you stayed there forever.

The car's lights lit up the early morning as it pulled up next to the living room's big bay window, overlooking the neighborhood. It sat there, waiting and watching for the sun to rise. Sarah Wilson sat inside the car, staring at the molotov cocktail sitting in her cup holder. Now, as memories of their life together flooded her brain at hyperspeed, Sarah found she could relax for a bit and cry for Randy.

She wept until the rays of the morning sun burned the dew off the car's windows.

"Rest in peace, my love," the grieving wife mumbled.

Wiping the snot from her nose with a sleeve of her shirt, Sarah picked up the beer bottle full of gas. She lit the paper stuffed into the bottle with a lighter, reached out of the car, and threw the bomb through the window of her house. She heard the glass shatter and the soft woosh of something igniting, and drove off. The ensuing explosion insured she would be saved from having to explain how her husband really fucking died. She turned up the radio. The oldies station was playing a seventies song about fine, sunshiny days. It surely was a beautiful morning.

Who's going to make Randy's Death Ziti? Sarah Wilson pondered as she drove to work one last time. *They better not fuck it up, or I'll put them in my hate-box, too.*

SIN RAFFLE

Thanksgiving Eve

Marquand couldn't cry. He could scream, but it wouldn't help. Even if he did, it wouldn't change anything. Nobody in the room would hear a goddamn thing but muffled, whispered grunting. He was muted by strips of silver duct tape covering his face from the mouth down to his throat.

"I would say this isn't personal, but we both know it is." Eddie, his captor, said before fumbling around Marquand's scrotum. Marq wondered if this was turning into a rape until something ripped his sack open. A burning fire shot through his groin. The shock of the trauma he endured had a numbing effect from the adrenaline coursing through his veins. As a result the initial slice didn't register in his mind, but his body reacted with a violent convulsion. Marq hyperventilated, each breath creating a sniveling, congested whine from his nostrils. He tried holding it back, but couldn't. He vomited so hard it spewed out his nostrils.

"Holy shit that's gross!" Eddie shouted, then a moment

later, "I can't believe the tape held. Damn. Glad I paid extra for heavy duty."

Marq's sinuses were filled with liquified salad and stomach acid, it burned the inside of his face. Unable to breathe, he was also suffocating and drowning in his own vomit. He lost the urge to fight back long ago. Marq knew he wasn't going anywhere, any time soon. Or ever again, for the matter.

Before the genital mutilation, Eddie plucked Marq's eyeballs out of his face with a stainless steel melon ball scooper. Marq squealed from behind the duct tape when the scooper first dug into his left eye socket with a click. It was so shrill, he shattered his vocal chords. Not as if he would ever need to speak again.

His abductor jumped Marq on the way home from the bar, striking him from the shadows of a long abandoned church. A blow to the head knocked him unconscious. He woke up restrained, taped to the chair in his own dining room. Marq's lover's husband, Eddie, hovered over him with an array of kitchen utensils at his disposal. Carving and paring knives sat alongside spoons, meat tenderizing hammers and a wired implement used for making shoe stringing potatoes. Andrea's husband was clicking the slicer on the melon ball scooper back and forth by Marq's ear. Marquand found out right away why. In this instance, it was the perfect implement for removing a person's eyeballs from their sockets.

He felt the duct tape pull away from his lips and a mouthful of green slime streaked with bile and blood fell onto his lap . Marq sucked in a gulp of fresh air. It was as succulent as a prime rib, and just as bloody. He sighed a gurgling moan as his bowels let loose and he shit himself. Black stool bubbled and squirted up between his legs, mixing with the remains of his genitals.

"God that's fucking gross. Jesus, you're nasty. I can't believe how much you fucking stink! What the fuck, man!" Eddie said. Marquand heard the desperation in the man's words. This was more than a crime of passion. It was revenge. "Maybe you'll be able to see better with these for eyes, you fucking prick!"

Marq felt something wet slap on his face. Though he was blinded, Marq saw each bolt of pain pierce through shifting ink blots of black and mottled gray. He stopped struggling, resolving he deserved the treatment. Marquand knew he was destined to die sooner or later, considering the severity of the crimes he, too, committed. It was fate, his own sins placed him here. The same crimes also secured him a slot in the lottery. He was certain if Eddie wasn't his executioner, the National Axeman would be at the Federal Gallows on New Year's Day.

Marq's limbs grew numb, then turned cold. As consciousness slipped away, he felt at ease. He saw his late son's smiling face welcoming him to the beyond.

Phillipe… He could swear he heard his son's name. But he knew it was impossible. He imagined the sound, a harbinger of the inevitable. Anticipation of death, he had learned in recent weeks, was worse than death itself. He was relieved to get the monkey off his back.

Sweat dripped off Eddie's brow. If murder was hard work, torture was laborious. Marquand, the son of bitch who was fucking Andrea, was duct taped to a chair in front of him. The adulterer's head lolled to a side, resting on his shoulder. His eyes didn't look right. Pink and dripping with blood, they gazed back, without pupils. He was dead, Eddie was certain of this much. Not many people could live through having their eyes plucked out, and their nuts stuffed in the empty sockets. Call it a self-tea-bagging, with some assistance by a jilted husband.

I just killed a man. Eddie thought, afraid to speak. What was he thinking? The insane portion of his mind came to the defense of the heinous act he committed. This was on her. Andrea caused this. *So what if I get thrown in the lottery?* He thought, *It was worth it.* He loved her and would do anything for their family, including sacrificing his own life. Families of the lottery winner were always set for life, the Government saw to it. Not to mention the lucrative talk show and television news circuit.

Sure, they'd have to answer questions like, *'Did you know he was a murderer?'* *'Why did he do this?'* and so forth. Sure, she'd endure far more intrusive questions, about their sex life and her own infidelity. But the kids would be set with more money than they could spend.

Eddie washed his hands in the sink. He didn't bother hiding the evidence. They, the powers that be, knew he did this, there was no hiding it. The Government knew everything you did. *Psi-Veillance* tech made it possible. Friends, family and other working slobs were the only people Americans could keep secrets from. Uncle Sam, on the other hand, well… he was always watching, always listening. He wasn't Big Brother, he was something more, and something less. From your internet use to what time you woke up to piss, PV cataloged it all. And if something you did was deemed illegal by the AI's in PV… you were put in the lottery.

The Government didn't call it a lottery. Gambling was, of course, illegal in 2068, and had been for the better part of two decades. No, they called it the Annual Sin Raffle. One person, each year was hung on national TV on the White House lawn. It was typically a murderer or child molester. But not always.

Eddie recalled how, in the lottery of 2050, the unlucky winner's infraction was a misdemeanor shoplifting charge. The upside of it all? At least the condoms the kid stole prevented him from conceiving more dumb asses. Oh, and it made his family rich.

Eddie washed his hands and face in the sink. He dried off with a clean towel, then he draped it over Marquand's face. The death mask of his wife's fucktoy was horrifying to behold. He couldn't believe he was capable of doing this to another living person. But he did do it. And he didn't like it, but exacting his personal vengeance on this man who made his wife turn from him gave him some satisfaction. He tapped his right temple, turning on his phone implant. A translucent screen opened up in his eye.

"Shopping list." Eddie commanded. The home screen brought up a list, written in Andrea's distinct hand.

Toilet Paper

Bottled Water

Something Ooey Gooey

What the fuck is something Ooey Gooey? He contemplated cutting out a piece of Marquand's brain and bringing it back to her. Or maybe running her lover's cock through a blender. He bet it would be *Ooey Gooey*. But Eddie thought better. He wasn't letting her in on his little rendezvous with her vaginal insert. He could, and would, play dumb until New Years Eve, when the National Executioners showed up at his door with handcuffs, a hood and a suitcase full of tax free money for the "survivors".

THANKSGIVING

"**M**ommy, if I don't do my homework, will I be put in the lottery?" Andrea's young daughter, Mia, asked her as they set out the dressings for Thanksgiving Dinner. Andrea didn't know how to answer the question. As far as she knew, not doing your homework wasn't a crime.

"No, honey. Whoever told you that should be ashamed of themselves."

"Sally, on the school bus!"

"Well Sally is mostly wrong, dear."

"What do you mean?"

"What I mean, honey, is it's not illegal, but following school rules prepares you for following the law, right?"

"That's what my teacher tells me."

"See, your teacher is wise. Sally, not so much. Sally's Mommy and Daddy probably had to tell her that, so she'd do her own homework."

"Probably, Mommy. Sally's a turd."

"Mia! That wasn't nice!" She watched her daughter blush in embarrassment.

"I'm sorry Mommy."

"It's okay, dear. Can you let your Daddy and big brother know dinner will be ready soon?" The little girl nodded and ran off, out of the kitchen. Along with her little helper, Andrea's roll-away buffet counter was filled with all the trappings of a typical holiday feast. The delicious aromas of sage stuffing, coleslaw, mashed potatoes, sweet potatoes, green bean casserole, cream corn and Lima beans, cranberry sauce (from a can!) and a deep roasted turkey breast, sliced, filled the room.

The chirp of Andrea's ringtone buzzed in her colloquial implant. She saw the caller ID in her eye. It was Jill from the office. "Answer phone." She said.

"Andrea?" Jill asked. Her voice had a serious tone.

"What's wrong Jill?"

"Marquand… he's…"

"What about Marq, Jill?"

"Oh, my God, Andrea. Marquand's dead! His body was found in his house today. Someone tortured him to death." Andrea gasped aloud. "Andrea, I heard from the EMT's someone plucked his eyes out and…"

"And what Jill?" Andrea spoke to slow down the

information dump. She was processing the details. Jill, her subordinate at the office, was on the phone with her. Someone murdered Marquand… Marq was dead. She fell into shock.

"Whomever it was, they…" Jill was having trouble saying it, "They cut his testicles off and put them in his eye sockets." Silence hung on the line. Andrea stood in her kitchen, staring at the stove, a blank look on her face. Absently, she started tapping her foot. She needed to take control of the situation before she lost it.

"When did this happen?" Andrea managed to keep her composure. She was an ice queen in stressful situations. *Don't ever let them see you sweat, right?*

"Late last night. My Lord, Andrea. Can you believe this? The bad luck he had this year, especially during the Halloween party. Do you think it's the same people who… I don't know, do you think they came back to finish what they started? The horrible things that happened to Lori and little Phillipe." She was frantic on the other end of the phone. It was annoying Andrea to no end.

"That's nonsense, Jill." She tried not to be condescending. It didn't work.

"I don't know, Andrea." Jill said in a meek voice after Andrea's verbal throat punch. "He was rich, and he was our boss. So you never know. There might've been some kidnapping ransom gone wrong thing going on here. Why else would they have tortured him so?"

"What's going on with the firm? Any word?"

"Your guess is as good as mine. Odds are we'll be unemployed."

"Thanks, Jill." Andrea closed the call, tired of hearing the graphic details of conjecture. Nausea set upon her. She bent over fighting for air. Mia came running back into the kitchen.

"Mommy, Daddy and dummy are ready!" The smiling girl saw right away something was wrong with her mother. "Are you okay Mommy?" Andrea stood up, gathering her composure.

"Yes, baby girl. Don't call your brother dummy, please. His name is Scott. Now, you go sit down at the table with them."

"Alright Mommy!" Mia ran to the dining room. Andrea, solemn, glum and still in emotional shock on the inside, put on her best holiday happy face. She placed both hands on the cart and squeezed until her fingers turned white, then red. She pushed the cart forward, followed her daughter and joined her family at the table.

CHRISTMAS EVE

Eddie and Andrea sat in their parlor, the lights of their Christmas tree twinkling in the otherwise dark room. They watched their children sleep on the living room flat-screen. Dual sleep-cams scanned the bedrooms of both children. Mia and Scotty were in deep REM sleep. They wouldn't wake any time soon. Their parents, however, were wide awake.

A half empty bottle of rye whiskey sat next to a pair of rock glasses, complete with melting ice cubes. Eddie leaned forward and poured the whiskey into one, then filled the other. He handed her the drink. She took it and swirled the ice about. The couple toasted one another by tapping glasses, and drank down the liquor. This was their life since Thanksgiving. Eddie and Andrea spoke to each other only when necessary.

"We should put the gifts under the tree before we drink anymore, Santa." Andrea said, placing the glass of ice back on the table.

"Let's go get them, Mrs. Claus." Eddie agreed. He put his glass down in suit, and stood up. The gifts were hidden in a loft in the garage. The couple made their way to the secreted cache. The stacked packages, wrapped in holiday color schemes, were labeled for one child or the other. Eddie and Andrea carried them to the living room, stacking them under the Christmas tree in piles declaring Mia or Scotty. There were no gifts labeled Eddie or Andrea.

Twenty minutes later, the couple were back on the couch, rock glasses full of rye whiskey in their hands. Eddie and Andrea stared at each other in silence as they drank. Thirty minutes later, the bottle was empty. With nothing better to do, they fucked. It was cold, emotionless, and fast. Neither of them made any sounds. When it was done, Andrea excused herself to use the bathroom.

Eddie remained on the couch, he closed his eyes and drifted off to sleep. Andrea, too, passed out. Her pants around her knees, curled in a fetal position at the base of the toilet. They both woke at the same time, with throbbing heads, fifteen minutes before their children rose to discover what gifts Santa left under the tree.

It wasn't how either of them expected to spend their last Christmas Eve together.

CHRISTMAS

A day of feasting came and went. Mia and Scotty got everything they asked Santa to bring. Scotty's Federal Gallows playset, complete with a real working trapdoor kept him busy for hours, hanging criminals. Mia's new Suzie Secrets doll was ready to listen to all of her surreptitious thoughts, and Mia whispered them all to her new digital recording confidant. All throughout the day they laughed and played with their new toys. It was a good day, a day to remember. Right up until the kids went to bed, and Eddie handed Andrea the gift.

She didn't take it.

"What's this?" She asked him.

"It's for you. I got you something." He took her hand and placed the little box in it.

"Eddie, we agreed no gifts." She wouldn't grasp the box.

"I don't care. I got you this before we made that agreement." Andrea gave him a stern look.

"I can't take it."

"What do you mean you can't take it? You're my wife, of course you can take a gift from your husband." He opened the box. A silver ring with a ruby stone glared back.

"No, Eddie, I can't take it. It wouldn't be right." She ignored the offering. Instead she kept eye contact with Eddie.

"Is this any way for a wife to treat a husband? Really? I don't ask for much from you, Andrea. I don't push issues with you over anything." He was starting to tear up.

"I know, but I can't take this, Eddie."

"Bullshit. You can. You just won't. I don't know what happened. You used to be happy. Now you don't talk to me unless it's required. I tell you I love you, you can't answer me, or you tell me thank you. It's bullshit. The kids can see what's going on."

"Not today, not now, it's not appropriate. It's Christmas."

"It's never a good time to talk, Andrea, or haven't you noticed? Have you ever once stopped to think that maybe we don't have the time to play these games? You're always thinking of yourself, I swear to fucking God."

"I'm not playing a game, Eddie. I'm unemployed, the head of the firm died at Thanksgiving, am I right? Why should I be festive? Give me one reason."

"You have us, you have your family! Just take it, for fuck's sake." He clenched his hand around hers, forcing her to hold the box and its contents. She took it and finally looked down at the jewelry.

"Eddie, it's beautiful. I don't have anything for you!"

"Andrea, all I want for Christmas from you…" he choked up, finding it hard to speak. He looked her in the eyes.

"Is what? What is it?" Her voice shook.

"All I want from you is my wife back. I've missed her. I've done everything I can do, now the rest is up to you." Eddie broke into tears. He lunged forward and embraced his wife, closing his eyes. She accepted him this time, but her eyes remained open, staring at nothing.

New Years Eve

"Ten!" The clock on the flat-screen counted down.

"Nine!" Eddie and Andrea, along with their children, screamed out the numbers with it.

"Eight!" As a family they watched the ball drop from Times Square.

"Seven!" It was a tradition in their house to let the kids stay up and watch the New Year ring in.

"Six!" They were like all their neighbors and everybody in America, for the matter.

"Five!" Everyone stayed up for the East Coast ball drop.

"Four!" They all wanted to see the drawing for the lottery.

"Three!" It came following the fireworks.

"Two!" In this household, someone feared they would strike lightning.

"One!" After the nature of their crime, it was inevitable.

"Happy New Year!" Eddie and Andrea kissed for the first time in a month. They held each other close. It would be the last time they kissed or touched.

The fireworks commenced over the Washington Monument. They lit up the flat-screen. The kids weren't watching it, though, their attention was to the windows. The Stone residence wasn't far from the nation's capital, so

Eddie didn't think anything of it. In years past, they could see the spectacle on cloudless nights.

"Look at the bright lights outside!" Mia said. It was true. It was too bright to be the distant fireworks. Through the windows of their house, they could see the late morning night was lit up. Drones with spotlights were flying everywhere. The President's seal replaced the fading fireworks on the flat-screen. The camera panned back, revealing the desk of the oval office, and the President himself, dressed in the black and red robes of his office. Andrea squeezed Eddie tighter.

"Ladies and gentlemen, the citizens of the United States of North America," the portly man paused. He smiled as he spoke and his bald head reflected the bright camera lights, creating a glaring aura about his face, "Tonight we honor the annual tradition started 40 years ago, to aid in the effort to reduce crime in our country. The Sin Raffle has done exactly what it was intended to, prevented crime. As a result, in 2068, we have no jails, no police, and most importantly, the lowest crime rate as a nation in the history of man. And now, following in the steps of our Lord and Savior, Jesus Christ, one citizen must pay for the sins of all."

Eddie broke away from Andrea's embrace. He knew what was happening outside.

"What are you doing?" She asked him.

"You'll see. Kids, come here, sit on the couch." They followed their father's instructions. Andrea sat with them.

"Daddy, Mommy, why are all the lights on outside at night?" Scotty asked.

"I think it's the Executioners for the lottery." Eddie told his son.

"Oh no! Mommy! You said they wouldn't come for me if I didn't turn in my homework!" Mia cried.

"They're not here for you, pumpkin." Andrea assured her daughter.

"Then who are they here for?" Her daughter asked. A loud knocking resonated on the door. Neither adult looked surprised. The kids, on the other hand, clung to their mother.

"I'm sorry, Andrea. I loved you so much, I had to." Eddie said.

"You had to… what?" She replied.

"What did Daddy do, Mommy?" Mia cried out.

"I, I don't," she stopped in mid-sentence, looking at her daughter and son. They were terrified, "what is going on Ed?"

"You know what I did. And I did it for you." He told her, his bottom lip shaking. A tear rolled down his cheek.

Marq… she mouthed without saying the word. Eddie nodded and opened the door. Andrea's expression turned from one of concern to rage. Her eyes bulged and her face turned red.

Eddie stood before the National Executioners; the High Executioner—a man in a black suit carrying a briefcase—and his enforcers, the National Axemen. The former resembled an undertaker, the others wore the traditional black hoods of the Axemen brotherhood.

"Good day, citizens. As you may know, I am the High

Executioner. It's my duty to issue a warrant for the arrest of the person drawn in this year's National Sin Raffle." He handed the briefcase to one of the Axemen. Long, waxy fingers pressed a pair of buttons and the case flipped open. Inside sat stacks of money, bound hundred dollar bills, and a certificate, embossed with the seal of the United States of North America. "Andrea Dawn Stone?"

"Yes," Andrea replied, her voice smooth and cold. Eddie looked at his wife, confused.

"What's going on? You're here for me, not her. She had nothing to do with it! I killed him, she only..." He stopped before saying too much in front of the kids.

"You stand accused of crimes against the people of the United States of North America. How do you plead?" The High Executioner asked.

"What?" Eddie interrupted. "Andrea? What? You're wrong! I did this! I killed Marquand Richardson, it should be me!"

"I plead not guilty, your honor." It was tradition for the lottery winner to plead not guilty. She bent her head down in shame and looked at the floor.

"So be it." He tapped his wrist with his fingers in a symmetrical pattern. "The evidence." He commanded. The house flat-screen changed images from the President's speech to something else. Andrea's PV reel from last Halloween played for all of America to see her sins.

Halloween

"I want your big cock in my mouth, now Marq!" The flat-screen's speakers screamed in the room. The late

Marquand Richardson of Richardson & Partners LLC, stood in a brightly lit bathroom. In the vanity mirror was Andrea's reflection. She was kneading her breasts through her blouse and camisole. Her nipples, hard and erect, poked through the thin, silky material.

"We can't, my family will be home soon. In fact I think I heard them pull up in the car. We have to get out of here and back into my office."

"Yeah, about your family." Her tone changed, opportunist Andrea surfaced for the world to see on the video feed.

"What about them?" Marq furrowed his brow, staring her down. She didn't blink.

"I think it's time we slimmed the playing field."

"What do you mean?"

"I mean, if something happened to your family, it would be easier for us to be together."

"But that would put you in the lottery. Shit, us just talking about this puts us both in the lottery. Stop it, Andrea. Stop it right now."

"So what. You know how many people are put in the lottery every day? And for murder?"

"No, I don't."

"It's got to be thousands, maybe even millions! Those are the odds I'm willing to take to be with you. And if it works, after the ball drops on New Year's, we'll take out my family, too. No baggage. Just you and me starting our lives over."

"Andrea, you're a cold bitch."

"It's why you love me. I get things done. I always have."

"Yes, but I love my child, too."

"The baby is three weeks old. You'll forget it soon enough. Don't you want this?" She unzipped Marq's pants and the view shifted to his large member. Andrea blew her lover on the flat screen in front of her family and every household in the country. The fellation lasted for fifteen minutes. Both of them were too lost in ecstasy to hear the racket outside of the bath. Someone else was in the house.

Marq bucked forward and sighed as he climaxed. Andrea remembered the moment well, the taste of Marq's semen, how he made her feel. She also remembered what happened next. Eddie was shocked to see the door to the bathroom fly open. Marquand's wife, Lori, stood with her swaddled baby in her arms, her face aghast.

"Marq?" She screamed, staring at her husband's flaccid penis hanging before his personal assistant's face. "I knew something was going on with you two, but in my own house?"

"Lori, this isn't…" He protested.

"Oh shut the fuck up, you coward," Andrea said, standing. "This is exactly what you think it is, you stupid cunt." Before his wife could react, Andrea hopped up and pushed Lori, hard. The blow sent the woman stumbling backward. She fell, clinging to her baby as she hit the floor. Her head landed on the solid brass doorstop, driving the metal into the base of her skull and knocking her out cold.

"Andrea, what are you doing?"

"Something you and I should have done last year when

we fell in love, before you knocked this bitch up!" Lori moaned on the floor. She was coming to. Andrea kicked her in the head and the moaning stopped. She picked up the swaddled baby with one hand like he was a loaf of bread. The baby began to wail and cry with a piercing pitch. She reached down and grabbed the prone woman by the ankle with her free hand. She dragged the woman into the kitchen, Marq fought with his pants, pulling up the zipper and fumbling with the belt notches. . He pleaded with her to stop.

"Andrea, please, the baby is innocent. Give him to me." Marq approached Andrea with slow, steady steps. He stopped when she smiled.

"I'm not going to hurt him, come on." Andrea countered. "But, you should know, the baby's baggage."

"He's not baggage, he's a human being."

"No, he's fucking baggage. He's something that will stand in our way."

"Fuck this, Andrea. Really. He's my son! What are you doing?" Marq demanded.

"What? Huh? I'm not doing anything. How about you?" Andrea's video doppleganger feigned ignorance as she unwrapped the little man and started taking his clothes off. She ignored his banshee wails, going about her business cool and calm. She wrapped the clothes up in the blanket and slid it to the side on the counter. The naked baby squirmed on the counter. She opened the cupboard below and pulled out the drawer to the trash compactor.

"Andrea! No!" Marq charged at her. She held him back

with one arm. He tried moving past her without much visual effort. Andrea smiled, holding her ground. Eddie watched in horror as Marq allowed Andrea to follow through with her plan.

"Oh stop, Marq, unless you want to be in the lottery, too. Wait, you already are." With her free hand, she dumped his wailing son into the trash and slammed it close with her knee, muffling the baby's cries.

"Andrea! No!" He flailed at his lover. She turned, and pushed him back, knocking him over a chair and slamming his head into the wall. He landed, stunned, next to his unconscious wife. Before Marq could recover and stop her, Andrea turned on the compactor.

Eddie tore his eyes from the flat-screen and looked at his wife. She had no expression he could read. It dawned on him, she was fucking evil. He couldn't move, couldn't speak. The sight of her made him sick. He felt nausea rising in his belly and was glad his mouth wasn't duct taped.

"Does this count as a third trimester abortion?" Andrea asked. Her expression was blank. The motor hummed and the sound segued from the desperate cries of a child to the whine of a motor being pushed to its limits. A loud pop followed and smoke billowed from the compactor's motor housing. At the sound, Marq jumped and stumbled back to the floor, frozen in shock. The kitchen filled with the scent of burnt oil. Andrea pulled on the handle, but the compactor wouldn't open.

"I guess you're not supposed to overstuff these things. You better call someone to check on that."

Marquand broke out of his catatonia and started wailing.

"Phillipe! Oh no, Phillipe! Andrea, what have you done, what have you done? Phillipe!" Marq cried, struggling as he rose from the floor. Tears streamed and snot blew bubbles out of his nostrils. He threw his hands over his face. Andrea pulled a long filet knife from a wood block. She marched to Lori's prone body.

"Time for Mommy to say goodbye."

"I can't let you…" Marquand said and rolled on top of his wife, shielding her from his murderous lover.

"You will let me, 'cause honey, I can't stop now. If the baby was a carry on, this bitch is way too much luggage." Andrea pulled Marq off Lori, he slumped on his side, weeping, covering his face with his hands. Andrea mounted the woman.

Eddie watched her raise the thin blade above her head, holding the handle with both hands. He didn't feel bad for killing Marq after witnessing how little he fought for his family. Eddie knew if Mia and Scotty were in danger, he'd give his own life for theirs.

"No!" Marq protested, again in vain. Eddie was getting sicker by the second at Marq's complacency. He said much, but did little to stop Andrea. He was as guilty as her in his passive aggressiveness. The Andrea on the screen rolled her eyes in her head, showing her disdain at his feeble demonstration of resistance. Eddie followed in suit.

"You're such a pussy Marq."

He reached his arms out to grab her, too late. Andrea

dropped the blade, plunging it into Lori's exposed temple. The woman's eyes popped open in response to a foreign object burrowing through her frontal lobe. She twitched once. The force of the blow snapped the blade just under the handle. Blood trickled out of Lori's tear ducts and a puddle of urine formed around her pelvis on the floor. Andrea looked at the snapped blade with curiosity, twisting it in her grip. She grunted, then added, "They just don't make 'em like they used to anymore, hah?" Marq's face was aghast. He held a shaking hand over his mouth. Andrea twisted Lori's head to look her in the eyes.

And sliced her throat, ripping it open.

Blood spurted in random directions in short arcs as the remnants of the jagged, broken blade furrowed through flesh, cartilage and vascular tissue. When she was done sawing a second smile under Lori's chin, Andrea tossed the broken knife aside. More blood flowed out of the edges of the wound, pooling onto the ceramic tiles and flooding the kitchen floor in crimson.

"See how easy that is? Now. Let's change, get this bloody crap off us and get back to the party before anyone notices we've been gone, ok? If we make it through New Year's, my family is next. Then we'll be together, baggage free, like we've always wanted. You thought I was kidding when I said I would do anything for us to be together."

The video stopped and faded to the Presidential seal.

New Years Day

"For crimes committed in the United States of North America in the year of our Lord 2068, including adultery, five counts of conspiring to commit murder, two counts of murder in the first degree, including the murder of Mrs. Lori Richardson and her infant son, Philippe Richardson, you are hereby ordered to be executed by the state. Do you have anything to say for your crimes, Mrs. Stone?" She turned to her family, her head bowed down in shame.

"I'm sorry, Eddie. I'm sorry Mia, I'm sorry Scotty. Mommy is sorry…" Her words faded into an inaudible whisper.

"Mommy was going to kill us?" Mia said. Everyone was ignoring the little girl except Eddie.

"Is that it?" The High Executioner asked Andrea.

"Mommy? Why were you going to kill us?" Eddie heard Mia plead. Andrea dismissed her daughter. Eddie didn't know how to answer her. He was too dumbfounded with the revelation, so he pulled her close to him and away from her mother. After preparing himself to be the one they came for, he was in as much shock as the kids.

"Yes, sir." Andrea extended her arms, her fingers cupped, her eyes still focused on the floor.

"No! Take me! Don't take her! I killed him for her! I did it! Me! Not her!" Eddie pleaded with the executioners. The National Axemen handcuffed Andrea.

"Daddy? Mommy?" Mia cried. He watched as Scotty remained silent throughout the whole ordeal, shaking his head, tugging his hair and bobbing to and fro from his seat. Eddie felt his heart break for the little boy.

"We are so very sorry for your loss, Mr. Stone. We

know you will find the coming days trying on your family, emotionally. Having lost partial income in the household, please accept this token of gratitude from your government."

"But you don't understand, I..." The Executioner cut Eddie off and handed him the briefcase, ignoring his protests.

"Yet I do understand, Mr. Stone. Please excuse us. We have an urgent matter to attend to at the capital, as I'm sure you are aware of."

Andrea, the Axemen and the High Executioner stepped away to a waiting hoverjet. The whine of its antigrav hoverfans resonated off the surrounding buildings. The foursome disappeared into the aircraft's gray hull and the door shut. Eddie held his children tight to his sides as they watched the National Executioners fly away with their family's matriarch, from the porch of their suburban Washington home.

Eddie took his children back inside. He closed the door and brought them to the couch. They sat together without speaking for a few minutes until the ever curious Mia broke the tension.

"Daddy? Why did Mommy do those things? She said she was going to kill us."

Scotty remained silent, drooling, his hair a twisted mess. Eddie knew his oldest child was destined for years of therapy, if he didn't take his own life first. How does a child accept their mother's threats to kill them, after witnessing her commit a vicious double murder? They don't.

"I don't know, Mia. I don't know," He turned off the flat-screen, they didn't need to watch Andrea's hanging, "I want you two to go to bed. We've got a busy day tomorrow." They didn't protest, both children went straight to their bedrooms.

He pulled the shades down. Outside, the neighborhood was starting to light up, again. News reporters were gathering en masse to interview the family of this year's Sin Raffle. He turned off all the lights in the house. For a while he sat in the dark, his body shaking from the adrenaline coursing through his veins, wondering what happened.

Why, Andrea? Why? He stopped himself. In hindsight, he didn't want to know the answer. It was better this way, he supposed, not knowing. Eddie looked at the briefcase on the table and remembered the money.

He stood, went to the case and opened it. It was there, more than his family would need until they all died. He thumbed his fingers through the bills. The smell of new paper money was fresh and crisp. He closed it, satisfied it was real. Something twinkled in the twilight. It was the ring Eddie gave Andrea for Christmas. She left it on the table before she was taken away. He slipped the ring on his pinky and walked into the kitchen. Ed opened up the drawer of utensils and rummaged through its contents. He withdrew a melon baller.

Eddie Stone threw the device, along with Andrea's Christmas ring, into the trash.

Thirty minutes later, Andrea Dawn Stone was led up the Federal Gallows on the White House lawn. A large crowd was gathered, all Washington dignitaries: Senators, congressmen, important judges and lawyers. She gazed at all of them here to witness her execution.

The National Axemen led her to a spot marked with a large X. One of the men placed a hemp noose around her neck and stepped aside. The High Executioner approached and stood in front of her. "Any final words, Mrs. Stone?" He asked. There was a brief moment, then Andrea nodded. "So be it, make your case." The High Executioner declared. Andrea smiled and coughed once, clearing her throat. "Marquand, my love." She took a deep breath and stared into the hard camera focused on the Gallows. "I did it all for you." She said, bold and defiant in her tone. The High Executioner nodded. "Alas, so be it." The Axeman placed a black hood over her head. The public needed to see her punishment, they didn't need to see her eyes bulge out of their sockets, or her face turn purple from asphyxiation if the fall didn't kill her. The National Anthem played and fifty-two seconds later, the Axeman pulled a lever. Andrea closed her eyes under the hood and saw her lover's smile in her mind. It faded into a spiraling abyss.

The trap door under Andrea's feet fell away. She remembered the family she left behind.

Eddie, Mia and Scotty, I'm so sorry, Mommy's sorry…

Andrea Stone hung in space for an eternity.

I'm sorry I didn't kill you first.

The eternity ended.

M.EN.TOR

Darkness and light. A blurry haze of twilight then disembodied words…

"When will he wake up? Does he hear us?"

"He should have a full recovery from the surgery."

Memories…

From his vantage point on the roof top, the sniper could see an insurgent fighter strapping what looked like a bomb to a child. He shook his head and part of him wished it wasn't happening, another part knowing what he would have to do, and more so, fully understanding what would overcome him. Since the war began, he wasn't the only soldier having to make a decision like this, one that would end a life, but save countless others. It was a simple fact, the cost of freedom is bathed in blood and no one, it seemed, was innocent in this or any other conflict. He resigned from his inhibitions and smiled, raised his rifle and zoomed the site in on the child. He adjusted the lens and the young boy came into focus, no more than 10 years old, a pawn in a bigger game he had no understanding of.

Regardless, the boy wasn't completely innocent. The fates had cast their die and gave the boy's soul to a soulless race, and for that alone he must die. The sniper enjoyed taking life, even if it had no soul, and felt pure bliss as he hovered the cross-hairs on the boy's head. This, in turn, set something else off, an all too familiar feeling that he couldn't resist; creating a new moment all together. The boy wasn't going anywhere, of that he was sure.

He pulled his Barrett back, dropped prone on the roof, quickly unbuttoned his trousers, whipped out his penis and began to masturbate as he stared at the sky above. Within moments he climaxed, soiling his hand and the surrounding area with semen. He lay there, his chest and belly expanding and contracting as he breathed, his brain washed in dopamine. Clouds floated above in the great expanse, a disturbing calm in the wake of what would soon be happening on the ground below. He couldn't move, he could only stare at the blue and white in the heavens above, for what seemed to be an eternity until his radio clicked with static.

"Guardian Angel, Bravo squad is headed your way. Please report."

"Fuck!" the sniper muttered under his breath, "Fuck, fuck, fuck!"

He broke from his trance. A dozen soldiers would soon be walking into a shit storm facilitated by a preteen explosion, and all because he had to get off. He quickly wiped his hand off, buttoned his pants and peeked over the rooftop. He immediately noticed, much to his chagrin, that both the boy and insurgent were gone. He scanned the horizon and down the clustered avenue of buildings. Nothing. He rose his sight and used the telescopic lens, still nothing. The child and his deadly party favor surprise had disappeared. The radio squawked again.

"Guardian Angel, please report. Is Delta Zone clean?"

"Charlie Omega, this is Guardian Angel. Delta Zone is not clean, I repeat not clean. Move with caution."

"Copy that Guardian Angel" was their reply. The sniper peeked back and saw the squad a few blocks from his vantage point. The kid could have been anywhere. Then he saw the insurgent come back into view; the rebel appeared to be leaving the very building he was on top of. The disillusioned freedom fighter noticed the squad and ran back into the building, once again out of his view. They were below him, of that he was sure. He quickly wrapped his sniper rifle in a blanket, hid it under a carpet, grabbed his assault rifle and made his way to the stairwell of the building.

Then there was nothing.

"Cut away the base of the skull and insert the connector to the cerebral cortex."

Russ awoke in a sweat, and realized he was in a hospital bed and that he had been dreaming. He was unsure if it was a nightmare. An attractive red-haired nurse in green Army scrubs stood before him. He had no idea how he got here.

"Welcome back to the world of the living, sunshine," the smiling ginger said, "you should have the world's worst cotton mouth right now."

She bent over him and tipped a freshly poured cup of ice cold water in his mouth. He coughed a little as some of it went down the wrong pipe, but to Russ, it was the best thing he had ever tasted.

"Don't try to move," she said as she stood back up. "I'll go get the doctor. She'll want to see you." And just like that, the perky nurse exited the room.

He combed through his memories, at least, those he could gather. Then it all started coming back to him. The words came into his mind and stayed there.

My name is Sergeant Russell Mahoney, he thought, I am an Airborne Ranger in the United States Army. The rest was a blur of memories on fast forward, racing through his head. He had volunteered for a DARPA program involving microchips and brains. His mind searched for words and Project M.EN.TOR surfaced. Russ reached up and felt bandages behind his left ear, realized it was covering up something foreign to his body, and correctly assumed that would be a chip slot complete with MENTOR chip. The chip contained the computerized data that had been Mahoney in the field. His thoughts were still as clouded as his vision, regardless, Russ was simply glad to be alive after a dangerous surgery. He missed his wife and children and tried to think of them as he closed his eyes and drifted back to sleep without speaking another word to the nurse.

The young boy, no more than two years old, pulled up his diaper and crept up on the sleeping kittens. A gift from his grandmother, they looked so innocent, and serene. One of them jerked and kicked a leg, causing the boy to cautiously stand back. Was it chasing an ethereal mouse in its sleep? The boy didn't know. He didn't care in the grand scheme of things. He continued to watch them, then curiosity got the best of him. He reached forward and clasped both cats by the throat, ignoring the razor-sharp claws that dug into his forearms and chest, squeezing until they stopped mewing and squirming in his grasp. Then he let go and surveyed what he had achieved, blood dripping from his arms. The kittens lay like he had found them, still and serene. But now their lifeless eyes, open and unblinking, stared forward, they no longer dreamed of chasing mice, or anything else for that matter. The toddler saw this and smiled with joy as he filled his diaper.

"You still with us, soldier?"

Russ woke with a startle. A woman that was

obviously a doctor stood before him, a chart in hand. "Pennoire" was printed on her general issue scrubs, her dark hair was pulled back into a bun and black glasses adorned her eyes. He recalled she was the doctor in charge of the project.

"There you are, back again. You look startled. Having nightmares?" the doctor asked.

"I think so, I can't remember them. I've been having a ton of nightmares since I came out of surgery."

Reassuringly, the doctor replied, "That's expected, Sgt. Mahoney."

Russ sat up in the bed best as he could and realized he had shit himself.

"Crap," he muttered under his breath. "Doc, I, uh, need my bed pan changed."

"Foxholes and hospital beds, Sergeant. Not only do they make believers out of atheists, they turn grown men into babies, crapping themselves."

Russ laughed in response. Wasn't that the truth? he thought to himself.

"I'll have the nurse help you when she gets back, I graduated from bedpans sometime during my residency," the doctor quipped.

"Gee, thanks. When can I get out of here? My wife and kids must be worried to death about me."

"They've been notified that you came through the procedure. A day or two and we'll make an assessment on that. I'm sure you want to see your family, but Uncle Sam invested a small fortune in your head."

"Did he ever. Biggest headache he's ever given me, too." Russ twisted his head and cracked his neck, wincing.

"Something he excels in, standard operating procedure and all that jazz," the doctor replied. "Your vitals seem fine, just let me know if you continue to have nightmares. It's most likely your brain adapting to the chip, processing the added information. That's what dreams are, they're your mind processing and filing what you've experienced during the day." The nurse entered the room with a selection of cleaning supplies. Dr. Pennoire continued as she moved toward the door. "You could think of your brain as an organic computer updating files when you sleep. And this is my cue to leave you and Katrina alone for some privacy."

"Gee, thanks," Russ returned, trying to have some humor.

"Any time, Sergeant." The doctor exited his room with these words.

"Let's get you cleaned up, soldier," the nurse told him as she snapped the cuff of a vinyl glove.

"Even better!" Russ joked and turned on his side so the nurse could do her job. "Watch where you stick those fingers!" he managed to laugh out.

The sniper made his way down the stairs, making an effort to cover the clap of his boots on the concrete. Within moments he was on the ground floor, rubble and broken furniture scattered about, providing cover to everyone and anyone who might be hiding. He stopped and bent to a knee, surveying the room. It was empty. Then there was movement. Unsure if it was settling debris or a suicide bomber, the sniper went prone, readying his weapon. He peeked his head around the corner of a half-burned credenza, and there stood the young boy, roughly 15 feet from him. The boy turned his head at the same moment and made eye contact with the sniper before he could hide. Like a body snatcher, he raised his hand and pointed in the soldier's direction.

The boy with a bomb strapped to his chest stood there, only pointing, not speaking, apparently shocked to see the sniper. Behind him stood another child, a girl clutching a doll, as well as the insurgent that had caused this mess. She saw the soldier and screamed, attracting the insurgent's attention. The rebel fighter turned and saw the sniper standing there with his assault rifle aimed at the boy. The insurgent pulled out a long kitchen butcher knife and charged the sniper, screaming "Allahu Akbar!"

The sniper turned his attention at the bladed threat.

"Good God! Wake up!"

Russ sat straight up in bed, bathed in sweat. His wife, Meghan, was hunched over him, a look of anxiety on her face.

"Meghan? What, what is it?" His mind was cloudy and his eyes found it difficult to focus.

"You had another nightmare, honey. Kicking in the sheets and screaming. This is the third since you got out of the hospital. You better call the doctor in the morning." She started to calm down. "Do you remember what it was about this time?" Meghan Mahoney's voice still shook, trying to sound confident and barely masking her concern for her husband.

"No, no I don't." Russ's head was full of cobwebs. He could never remember the dreams that tormented him. He wished he could, perhaps then they would go away. His wife pulled the sheets up and held him tightly. Reassured and comforted by her presence, Russ drifted back off to sleep.

Blood flowed and glistened on the mahogany finish of the piano, slowly spreading out from the bludgeoned head that had been smashed into it. The pulpy mess was still attached to a body, which sat limp on the piano's bench; its arms hanging lifeless, blood running down over the keys and dripping down the extremities and off the corpse's fingers into myriad pools on the floor.

"What did you do to your music teacher?" screamed the hysterical woman in a sundress.

"I killed the faggot, Mother," the teenager replied, an electric guitar hung loosely in his hand. Both the teenager and the guitar were covered in gore and bits of brain matter.

"Watch that language, young man! This is serious, we won't be able to protect you this time!" She was grasping at her hair, tears raining from her eyes. "The cats and dogs were one thing, but this?"

"But he touched me in a bad way, Mother, in a faggoty way." He emphasized the made-up word. "What else was I supposed to do?"

"Get me, get your father!" She grasped her son by the shoulders and began shaking him so violently he dropped the guitar with a thud. "But don't kill a person! What are we going to do? What are we going to do with you?"

He stood there silent, listening to his mother rant and spit in his face, showing no emotion, a facade that hid his elation at taking the life of a person for the first time. He viciously grabbed his mother and shook her in return, as euphoria coursed through his veins.

"Nothing!" he screamed back in her face.

It was glorious, and the rush made his dick hard. His mother's mouth opened to speak.

"My God! My God! What are you doing?"

Russ found himself standing in his dining room, Meghan's shoulders clenched in his hands. She was haggard and distraught, tears streaming down her face.

"What's going on?" Russ was confused and bewildered. Had he been sleepwalking?

"I found you standing in the kitchen just staring," Meghan managed through the tears that still streamed down her face. "You wouldn't answer me and when I touched you, you grabbed me and started shaking me."

"My God" was all he could utter.

"Did you call the doctors like you said you would?" she inquired, gathering her composure.

"Yes, I left a message with the answering service this morning."

"Well, I hope they call back tomorrow. This is concerning me. It's almost every night now!"

"Shhhh…" Russ said and tried to hug his wife.

"Don't shush me! This is serious!" She slammed her fists into his chest, pushing him away.

"You're not shushing for me, it's for them." Russ gestured to their young son and daughter, both of whom had heard the disturbance and had come to see what Mommy and Daddy were fighting over. The duo looked on, hiding around the edge of a cabinet. Russ and Meghan stared back at their children with nothing to say. They held one another tightly as tears mutually streamed from their eyes.

"Sleepwalking could certainly be a side effect of the procedure, Sergeant Mahoney." Dr. Pennoire spoke into the phone, calm and direct in her speech, assuring Russ that what he was experiencing was expected and normal and would go away as his brain continued to heal, "I must remind you that you are not fully recovered, you've only been home four days and had the procedure less than a week before that."

"Well, I just wanted to let you know what was going on," Russ admitted.

"And we appreciate that. It's doubtful you would have a serious incident as a result," the doctor answered.

"And shaking my wife in my sleep isn't a serious incident? I'd damn sure say it was, Doc." Russ was becoming agitated.

"We can understand that you feel that way, but she shouldn't have touched you while you were in that state, she should keep this in mind going into the future," she advised.

"Yes, Doc. Thanks. If anything else happens I'll call." Russ wasn't assured by her words.

"Absolutely, Sergeant. Good day." And she hung the phone up. Russ stared at the dimming screen of his cell phone wondering if he had made the right decision in volunteering for this secret project.

The insurgent came at him with the knife, the blade catching a glare of light that poked in through the broken windows of the building's basement. Time seemed to nearly stop as the knife came plunging at him. He realized in that frozen moment it was a woman, something hard to decipher the way these heathens dressed, but a woman all the same. She was on him like lightning, pushing him to the ground. As he fell back, he squeezed the trigger of his Colt and bullets sprayed the room in slo-mo. A burst of rounds plowed into the plaster walls and ricocheted off concrete.

The random bullets nearly cut bomber boy and dolly girl in half, sending their mutilated bodies sprawling like pinwheels from the force of the lead slamming into their small bodies. He watched as they writhed from multiple impacts. He saw their agony as the hot metal pierced their flesh, each wound producing more blood than you thought their small bodies would contain. And he liked it.

Then he felt the insurgent's blade as it plunged into his chest and time caught up with him. He certainly did not like this. She was screaming something he couldn't understand as she tried pulling it back out, but the edge of the butcher knife was stuck on his rib cage and his lung was being pureed as she twisted it back and forth. Frothy, pink blood began to spurt up and out of the wound, covering them both in a bath of crimson.

Gore now covered his face as they struggled, stinging his eyes as he gasped for breath out of one lung. Then, as suddenly as it had begun, the fight was over. The woman was pulled back off him, kicking and screaming, and he saw the squad of American soldiers spread throughout the room. A medic ran to his side and started treating his wound.

"Stay with us, soldier!"

Russ woke in the hospital, again. This time was different. He was handcuffed to the bed and tubes were stuffed down his throat. It was painful to breathe, he noticed, and as much as he wanted to cough and clear his throat, he couldn't. He could barely move his head, but with effort he looked over and saw he was on a ventilator. What was going on? He tried speaking but the tubes prevented it, and all that came out was a grumbled moan.

He saw that redheaded nurse was in the room, adjusting a morphine drip IV attached to his arm. She must have heard him groan, and could now certainly see his eyes were open as he stared at her. She stopped what she doing and left the room on a mission, as if something was wrong. Russ had barely processed this as Dr. Pennoire, now wearing a power suit and lab coat and accompanied by a pair of armed M.P.'s in dress blues, strolled into his room.

One of the soldiers, a black woman who's visage was the epitome of resting bitch face, closed the door behind the other M.P., a white guy with a serious case of acne scarring and a matching expression. Russ couldn't understand why they were there or why he was handcuffed. He tried to raise a chained hand, and as he did, Resting Bitch Face raised her rifle.

"That won't be necessary, stand down, Corporal." The doctor told her and the soldier did as ordered, snapping back to parade rest.

"You're awake, that's good," the doctor said. "If you can understand me, blink."

Russ blinked.

"Good. I want you to know you are restrained for your own safety, Sergeant. Do you understand?"

He blinked again.

"Now, typically, I'd ask what the last thing you remember was, but I regret if we allowed you to speak, your lung would collapse. So I'll cut to the chase. There has been a tragedy, likely as a result of your participation in the M.EN.TOR program."

Russ looked at her with as much inquisitive concern as his face could muster. The last thing he remembered was going to bed the night before. What had they done to him? Where was his family? Why were the guards here?

"There's no easy way to tell you this, but your children are dead, Sergeant Mahoney."

Russ felt his heart start to pound in his chest, and began to fight with his restraints. How had this happened? What was going on?

"You murdered them, shot them multiple times with an assault rifle from your private collection," the doctor replied matter of factly. "Your wife stabbed you in the chest before you could shoot her. You're only alive because our response team that had been monitoring you was able to pull her off you."

Russ stared blankly at the physician. He couldn't believe the words. His mind went blank. I killed my children? The thought made him want to die. He heard the life support machines start to increase in activity as his heart began to race and his blood pressure raised. He tried to process what he had been told and was finding it a difficult pill to swallow. The doctor said nothing more, and the room was silent but for the repetitive swoosh of his respirator and frantic beeps of the vitals monitor. Then the door opened, and Corporal Resting Bitch Face stepped aside to allow the nurse back into the room. She quickly went back to her duties that his waking moments had interrupted.

"Don't worry, Meghan's safe and will remain so," Dr. Pennoire continued. "She also thinks you are dead. And for all intents and purposes, you did die, and were brought back, so the lie isn't totally untrue."

Russ couldn't handle much more of this. He struggled more and more with the handcuffs, shaking the bed.

"Uncle Sam invested too much money in you, Sergeant Mahoney, for them to just let you die. You've got some very important work ahead of you."

The nurse turned up his morphine drip and he felt the narcotic course through his veins, sending him back into slumber.

The sniper laid in the surgical tent, unable to move. He was weak from blood loss and found breathing to be the hardest thing he could do. A tight bandage overflowing with gauze was wrapped around his chest. He was surrounded by a team of doctors when a woman accompanied by a pair of soldiers entered. She was dressed in a white lab coat with the name "Pennoire" emblazoned on the breast. In her hand was a file, and he saw his name and pay grade, LEE, DALLAS, E-5. Another man, a doctor perhaps, spoke up.

"He was stabbed in the chest by an insurgent making I.E.D.s just about an hour ago. They got him back here stat but he's lost a lot of blood."

"That's fine," the woman replied. "He's a perfect candidate for the mnemonic enhancement torrent, his skill sets are priceless. His confirmed kills make Chris Kyle look like a rookie. I'm slightly concerned with his psych profile, but we won't know its effects on the host Apprentice until after the pairing." Dr. Pennoire looked down at sergeant Dallas Lee, US Army sniper, and part-time psychopath, who had murdered kittens and music teachers before becoming a feared member of the Special Forces. She caressed his brow with her hand.

"Prep him for surgery, he doesn't have much time. The cerebral download can still work for the M.EN. TOR chip after his body shuts down, provided we keep the brain alive." She checked his pupils with a light pen as she spoke, then looked him the eyes. He looked back, coughing and choking as bloody phlegm dripped back down his throat from his mouth. "Part of you, Sergeant Lee, is going to live forever."

YETI SHIT BLUES

Everything you're about to read is true. It may not have happened in the precise order presented, and some of the players might have had different interpretations of said events. Not even the names of the participants have been changed. If you're one of the guilty parties enshrined in this, and want to get mad or angry, just sit down, shush and enjoy. Nobody is going to believe this bullshit, so what makes you think they'll believe you exist?

"Did they visit you yet?"

"Did who visit me, Joe?"

"The Men in Black."

"The fuckin' what did you just say?" I held the phone away from my ear, no longer interested in what Joe was telling me. He was batshit crazy, just shy of a tinfoil hat and straight jacket. Multiple trips on the LSD Light-Bright train did fucked up things to a person's mind. One of them was making you think imaginary men in black were after you.

"The men in black, they stopped me today. Told me, us, to stay away from the quarry." His voice rattled in the speaker of my phone.

"The quarry, where we went last weekend on your wild goose chase?"

"It was a serious investigation, measuring the psychic funnel of the blight."

"The psychic funnel I couldn't see? The imaginary event that caused your 'witch' with ESP to fall to the ground and have a fake seizure?"

"It wasn't fake. I told you it's a blight, an evil place. She couldn't take it."

"Okay, Joe. It wasn't fake. And—" I stumbled over her name, "What's her face, there," What was it? Oh, Starr, and she was about as fake as a modern neo-pagan witch could be. She wasn't shy about how she paid the bills. Starr worked at a lingerie modeling studio in Syracuse, a place where they did a little bit more than model for the right tips. Joe didn't wait for me to recover my train of thought.

"Her name is Starr. And she has ESP."

"She sure does." Placating Joe was often the best recourse, but I couldn't with this woman. Starr was something else. "She also told us a sasquatch shits on the lawn of her family's trailer."

"It was a Yeti."

"How the fuck could it be a Yeti? We're in New York, not the Himalayas!"

"It's the same cryptoid, Rick. Just do us both a favor. If

they talk to you, tell them you don't know anything about the quarry."

"Sure, Joe, I'll play stupid." I patronized him. I knew no men in black were ever coming. And the events surrounding the explosion at the Fenton Rock Quarry, almost two decades ago, were public knowledge. The cops didn't want people going up there for one reason: the ground was toxic. It was a simple deduction. Joe mistook a couple of plain clothes detectives for the legendary harbingers of the unknown. I should know, I'm a high end bodyguard.

A living weapon.

I didn't have time for this, Dee Dee and I had a date. I clicked off the call and threw my cell phone on the passenger's seat of my '71 Mach-1 Mustang. I shifted the car into gear and went from zero to sixty-five in less than ten seconds. I could afford a classic car of this caliber, keeping people like Benny Mardones, the Fishman guy in that acid drip band or any of the Baldwins alive when they came to the area. Men with my skills were always in demand.

I hauled ass down Route 104 to her dorm at Fenton University on the shore of Lake Ontario. I met Dee Dee at the gun show in April. The raven haired Lebanese beauty's enormous tits were eye magnets. Lucky for me I met her brothers, Hani and Farez, first. They weren't fans of any men ogling their little sister. This gave me the luxury of being the first guy to look her in the pupils when talking to her. Naturally, it led to us dating. Having a hot car didn't hurt my chances. Plus I think I'm the only man outside of her family to know she has gray eyes.

I found Dee Dee sitting on a bench near the shore. Tight jeans and a tighter sweater gave her the allure of a pin-up model painted on the nose of a B-52 in WWII.

"Hey, baby." Dee Dee said to me as I bent over to kiss her before sitting. To my surprise, she grabbed my jock. Two months of hanging out and I never pushed the sex issue, but damn, did she do it today. I reached a hand under her sweater and found the underwire of her bra. The buck stopped there. She pulled back. "No, no, no. Stop, please." She pulled the sweater down, covering the exposed olive skin of her midriff.

"Sorry, baby. I just thought…"

"It's okay baby." She squeezed my junk through my jeans. "You can't touch. You know that." Did I ever know it. "But, you know, I have an idea."

"Oh? What's that?"

"It's Friday, no?" I agreed with her. She smiled. "So why don't we get married today and get divorced on Monday?"

"What? Are you crazy Dee?"

"Well, yeah. I'm Lebanese! Of course I'm crazy. Let's go to the judge, get married, then we can fuck all weekend and I won't go to hell. We can get the wedding annulled on Monday because you won't convert to Islam. Pretty simple. Don't you think?"

She made sense, I mean I couldn't argue with her logic.

"Sure. Let's do it." She unzipped my pants and pulled

them down. My unit stood at attention. "What are you doing?" I asked, knowing fully *what* she was doing.

"Call this a taste of what's to come…" and she went about performing what I can only call the world's best oral sex, bringing me to an almost instant climax and finishing with a smack of her lips, while not losing a drop.

"Ahhh. You taste like honey." She rolled the 'n' on her tongue with a part of me helping the effect. "Let's go. The courthouse closes at 3:00." She grabbed my hand and we made a dash for my car, fumbling away as I pulled my pants up in stride. And that's how Dee Dee became Mrs. Rick Hawn for seventy-two hours, but it wasn't a honeymoon. Not one bit.

The ink was still wet on the marriage certificate when Dee Dee and I left the courthouse, ninety minutes later. We opened the glass doors and ran to my Mustang. I stopped, opened the door for her, and saw them half a block away, leaned up against a black sedan with tinted windows. They saw me, too. I knew who it was but couldn't believe it.

Joe's men in fucking black.

I pretended not to notice them walking toward us. My heart pounded in my chest and butterflies set my belly off kilter, but I got in the car. I turned the ignition and drove off, leaving them behind. Dee Dee didn't waste any time. She went back to fondling me through my jeans. I was so scared of the men in black, my wonder worm wasn't all too wonderous at the moment. Dee Dee caught on real quick.

"Is everything okay, baby?"

"Oh yeah, it will be when we get someplace alone."

Her frown turned back into a smile and she buried her head into my shoulder. My mind slowed into a moment of clarity. *Holy shit, this all meant Joe was telling the truth!* And it meant crazy ass Starr was on their naughty list. I had to warn her, like Joe warned me. So I hatched a plan on the spot.

"Hey baby. Wanna do something kinky on our way to the casino?"

"Sure baby. what did you have in mind?" Dee Dee asked.

"Ever been to a lingerie parlor?" I asked her…

"**P**rostate Massage, $60. Golden shower, $40. Glass Plate Job $80." I read the services provided by Sitting Pretty, listed on a chalkboard on an easel. "What the fuck is a glass plate job?"

"If you don't know, you don't want to know." Rob, the front desk manager of Sitting Pretty said.

Fair enough. Discipline $50. So why is a Boudoir photo shoot $200?" Shocked at the apparent price gouging, I asked Rob. He grunted in response to a question I didn't intend for him to answer. "What do you think, babe? I want something to remember this weekend with." The sign behind Rob declared lingerie and adult novelties were for sale. Hidden in the seedy heart of Syracuse, New York's north side, the place wasn't what you would call luxurious. But it was clean.

"I'm down with it baby. Anything. This is your weekend." She pinched my ass and I handed Rob the money. He led us to a private dressing room a short distance from the lobby.

"Your photographer will be in soon." He said, and left us to our privacy. The room was stocked with all different sizes and styles of lingerie in a rainbow of colors.

"This is different." I told Dee Dee.

"It sure is." She pushed me on the heart shaped bed in the center of the room, pulled her sweater off, releasing her breasts from its wool confines. A lacy black bra was all that remained to restrain them. "Get naked, boy!" She commanded and pulled her own shoes and jeans off. The panties matched the bra. Dee Dee planned this. I followed suit, stripping down to my boxers.

She jumped on top of me, dry humping away, rubbing her groin into mine. Dee Dee liked to be in charge. I wasn't going to argue with her. She pulled her panties aside and was about to consummate our marriage when Starr walked in the room.

"We can't fuck in here, guys, I'm sorry." She said. It killed the moment. "Hey, aren't you Rick?" She added, killing the moment even more.

"How does she know my husband?" Dee Dee asked, still on top, staring me down with her gray eyes.

"Husband? You never told me you were married." Starr said innocently.

"Of course he didn't." Dee Dee's massive boobs swayed to and fro in front of my chin. I turned my attention to them for a second and Dee Dee slapped me. "Wrong eyes, husband. I asked, how do you know this whore?"

"Excuse me? I'm not a whore. I met Rick last weekend at the Quarry." Starr wasn't helping my cause one bit.

"The Quarry? Where the kids party and make out?" Dee Dee crawled off me and pulled her clothes back on. "You son of a bitch. You take your new wife to one of your whore houses?"

"When did you get married?"

"You didn't even tell this bitch? You know what's going to happen to you when my brothers find out?"

"What are you talking about Dee Dee? She was with Joe. We only got married an hour ago."

"She said she was with you."

"I know she did. But she was with Joe. Speaking of which, Starr, have the men in black talked to you yet?"

"Who?" Dee Dee and Starr said in unison.

"The men in black. They talked to Joe, about the Quarry."

"What about the Quarry, Ricky? What were you two doing up there? Who are the men in black?" Dee Dee demanded answers to her questions. All I wanted to do was shake her like I was a bad parent and she was a toddler. And poor Starr was lost.

"I don't know what you're talking about, Rick. All I know is I'm never going back to that place again."

"I know where I'm not going!" Dee Dee shouted. I looked at her. She pulled her hair back into a ponytail. "No place with you!" She stormed out of the room, slamming the door behind her.

"What the fuck just happened? Did my wife just leave?"

"Looks to be that way," Starr confirmed, staring at me, smiling. I realized I was still naked. It took me a minute to get dressed. By the time I made it to the parking lot, Dee Dee was pulling away in an Uber.

And, of course, a familiar black sedan was sitting at the light kitty corner to the parlor. It raced past the building and followed Dee Dee. Not believing my eyes, I ran back inside the parlor. Starr was up front with Rob, both of them perplexed.

"What's up with this men in black thing? Also, we still have forty-five minutes left on your boudoir shoot." Starr said as I approached the desk.

"I don't care about the boudoir. And as far as the men in black go, I think they're out front right now. I don't know what they want, but I do know they freaked Joe out and they've been following me around town all day. Something to do with the quarry."

"They've been sent to silence us by the dark side. I need to go to my house. I've got protection for us there. It should get rid of them. Can you take me there?"

"Okay. Sure. Where do you live?" I didn't believe a thing she told me, but after the appearance of the men in black, I wasn't going to take any chances. Fake witch. Real witch. It couldn't hurt to cover all the bases at this point.

"The other side of Fulton, near Central Square and Constantia."

"Well, I gotta go back to Fenton anyway, and that's on the way, so this works out perfect." I looked out the door.

I was relieved to see the sedan was nowhere to be seen. "Come on, let's go!"

An hour later, I was turning off Route 3 onto a gravel road in the middle of nowhere. The sun set on the way out, and the headlights of my Mach-1 cut a pair of conical beams through a fog of flying insects. The rural highway weaved a path through the woods, almost resembling a tunnel of trees. Starr didn't say a goddamn thing on the ride out. She scrolled through her smartphone, looking at Lord knows on whatever social media platform. Until we pulled into the Shady Lane trailer park, nestled deep in the ass crack of Oswego county.

"Watch your step. He likes to shit alongside the driveway. And it's nasty. Makes babyshit smell like a birthday cake." *Birthday cake? Who was she talking about?* Her dog, her brother? Her father or mother? Stupid me had to ask…

"Who's that?" Before I remembered, it all coming back to me as she spoke.

"The Yeti." I held back from correcting her. *Yetis don't live in New York. Right?* "Turn here!" Starr startled me, my heart pounded in my chest. I cut the wheel hard right and pulled into the driveway to her trailer. I parked the car and we went inside. Lucky me, I didn't step in any Bigfoot crap. I didn't see or smell anything, either. It was dark.

The airtight interior smelled like cat piss and patchouli. The decor was much as I expected. Dreamcatchers and pentacles hung from random spots on the ceiling. The panel walls were covered in weird art. Starr went into another room. I stayed put. The last thing I wanted to do was be alone in a bedroom with this crazy broad. She came back out a moment later with a little, black backpack. I wasn't about to ask her what was inside it.

"I'm all set." She said as a pair of headlights lit up the driveway.

"Were you expecting company?"

"No. You think it might be the men in black?" Starr asked. *Wasn't she supposed to have ESP?* I wondered if she knew all this was going to happen ahead of time.

"I don't think they'd be shining lights on us like this." We heard the vehicle shut off and a sliding door rattle open. I peeked out a window. It was a white creeper van with tinted black windows.

"What is it?" Starr asked. *Don't you know?* I wanted to say. But didn't.

"A van, but I don't see anybody." On cue we heard her screeching voice.

"*Ricky! Come outside with your whore! Or we'll just shoot the place up!*" Dee Dee screamed, followed by the distinct sound of guns being cocked.

"Oh, shit! She brought her brothers!" I didn't have a single firearm on me. We were fucked. I didn't even have a knife to bring to this gun fight. I looked around, and saw a dagger sitting on what looked to be an altar. I slid it up the sleeve of my jean jacket. "Is there a backdoor on this thing?"

"Yes, down here." She led me to the back of the trailer and its emergency exit door. We popped it open and dropped outside. We crouched down. The grass was wet with condensation. "This way!" She whispered and led me around the back of the trailer. The farting sound of a couple of submachine guns on full auto echoed through the trailer park. I pulled Starr to the ground. Bits of fabric, insulation, glass, tin, plastic and everything else put into a house trailer flew about and stray bullets streaked above our heads. It lasted for a few minutes, until they ran out of ammo. It went quiet. Random pieces of the trailer fell to the ground and clunked. I waited a few more moments, and stood up, surveying the damage. The trailer was fucked.

"Hope you don't owe too much on that thing. I'm pretty sure they totaled it." I said.

"There they are!" A man with a thick accent shouted. I saw someone come around the side of the trailer. It was Dee Dee's brother Farez. With an Uzi, loading a fresh clip.

"Come on!" I grabbed Starr by the arm and we ran. Farez raised the nose of the weapon. It erupted with fire and thunder, lighting up the back yard. The submachinegun's bullets tore up ground with nine millimeter lead divots, chasing us around the corner of the prefabricated building.

"Fuck-ah you, you-ah bastard! No one cheats on-ah my sister with a *whore*!" Farez screamed. We rounded the other side of the trailer and bounded into the neighbor's property. I stopped and looked. No one followed. We ran seventy-two feet down the side of the neighbor's double-wide. I peeked around the edge of their faux-wood porch and saw my car sitting at the edge of the driveway, straight ahead. Dee Dee and her brothers were on the other side of their van. They couldn't see us.

I looked at Starr and counted with my fingers... one... two... three... we dashed to my Mach-1. I was two steps away when I discovered the single most disgusting, vile and straight up nasty pile of Lord knows what to ever exist.

It could have been the infamous Sasquatch poo. I wasn't sure. Whatever it was, the pile was a meter tall. I stepped into it, and sunk half way up my calf before I realized what happened. My sneaker and jeans were covered in shit. And the smell was horrible. It reeked of fetid meat and rotten eggs, with an undercurrent resembling a freshly opened box of Saturday morning sugar cereal.

"What the fuck!" I shouted out loud, gagging.

"I told you to watch out for Yeti shit by the driveway!" Starr berated me. "That sneaker is ruined. The jeans you might be able to save. I wouldn't get in the car. You're going to stink it up."

"*There they are!*" We heard Dee Dee screech.

"A little too late for that!" I opened the car door and we piled in. I turned the ignition and gunned the engine in reverse. The headlights lit up the front of the trailer. Farez and Hani stood side-by-side behind Dee Dee, reloading their Uzis. She was pointing at us like she was Brooke Adams or Donald Sutherland in Invasion of the Body Snatchers, her mouth twisted open. Behind them a dark shadow rose up, towering over the trio. I watched one brother fly into the air and skip across the neighbor's roof. The other brother launched into the windshield of their minivan, but not before getting off a blast of rounds from his Uzi. As I swung the Mustang out of the driveway, I saw the muzzle flash of the submachine gun light up the apelike features of a giant primate with a conical head. It was growling, showing long tusk-like fangs.

Holy shit, I'll be a son of a bitch! It was a Yeti!

"See! I told you! That bitch is gonna get fucked up. Shoot my trailer up with machine guns? Fuck you!" Starr flipped out her middle finger and taunted Dee Dee. I didn't feel bad for my wife one bit, knowing her time with the Yeti wasn't going to be fun. I think I heard Dee Dee scream one last time as we drove off. I pushed the pedal to the floor and we set out to find Joe and break the curse of the men in black. Oh, and change my jeans. Damn that shit stunk.

It was nearing midnight when I pulled up on the front lawn of Joe's small house. Out front stood a pizza delivery guy shaking his head. Starr hugged her pack and we walked up to the front door.

"You hit a skunk?" He asked. I pretended not to hear him. He pushed the issue. "You friends of this guy?" The pizza man asked us. I nodded in agreeance. "Can you bring this into him. It's paid for. I've come here three times to deliver it and all he does is stare at that light." He was acting strange, like something was bothering him.

"Okay, I guess… what light?" I said.

"I don't know. He's not my friend. He's yours, you said so yourself, I've gotta get out of here." He handed me the pizza box. I took it and the driver ran off to his car and drove away before we reached the stoop.

I knocked on the door. We waited a few minutes for Joe to answer. He didn't. I peeked into the window and sure as shit, there he was, staring at a Tesla orb. The lighting arced and traced about the interior surface of the ball of glass. And Joe stood there, staring at it.

I turned the door knob and it opened. Starr followed me into our mutual friend's home. He didn't acknowledge us. Light music played in the house, it had an ethereal feel to it. Soothing. Hypnotic.

"I don't advise looking at that light too long." I told Starr. But it was too late. I heard her backpack drop to the floor. She was standing next to Joe, in a similar catatonic state, staring at the ball of lightning. "Really? What the fuck." I pulled Starr's dagger out of my sleeve and threw it at the Tesla orb. The ball of glass shattered. Lightning arced out, bouncing off Joe and Starr, then faded away. My friends came out of their trance.

"Rick? Starr? What are you doing here?"

"Yeah, where am I?" Starr asked. She looked at Joe.

"Don't you remember?" I asked them.

"Remember what?" They said.

"Why we're here." I said. It was becoming clear to me the Tesla orb had a nefarious purpose. *Did it wipe their minds of memories?* I wondered.

"Oh, the pizza! It came! I'm so hungry!" Joe declared, and he, along with Starr started filling their faces with slices an eighteen inch New York City style pepperoni pizza.

Me? All the excitement took my appetite away. Besides, I smelled like a ripe skunk dipped in elephant diarrhea after stepping in the Yeti shit.

Instead I stepped outside to have a smoke and work on catching cancer. I tapped the pack of cigarettes, packing them down. I flipped open the top of the box, slid a bone out and brought it to my lips. A Zippo strike later it was lit. I inhaled a long drag and released a giant cloud. When it dissipated, I saw a black sedan parked next to my Mach-1.

"*Son of a…*" Two men, dressed in black suits, hats and sunglasses emerged from the car. They floated across the lawn to me. I smoked my cigarette like nothing was happening. Did I say they floated across the lawn? Making sure. They stopped an uncomfortable space away from me. Their faces were gaunt and stretched thin. I blew a cloud of smoke in the air between us. They stood, stoic and unmoving. The cloud faded away. "If you plan to ask for a few minutes to talk about your Lord and Saviour, I'm going to stop you right now. We don't give a fuck."

But we give a fuck about you, Rick. I heard in my head.

"I don't know nothing."

Of course you don't.

"If I don't know nothing, why am I still looking at your…" I paused and squinched my eyes and cheeks. "Faces?"

We'd like to offer you a job.

"A job?"

Yes, a job. Some of our demands are a bit more mundane than the spiritual events you witnessed at the rock Quarry – In unison, the duo wrinkled their noses. If they were noses. They were more like slits – *or the cryptoid inhabiting the local forests.*

"You mean the Yeti?" They nodded together. "Do you two do everything together?" They nodded, again. "Okay. What's this job?"

There's a computer programmer hiding in the Swiss Alps. We believe he caused the voting machine disruption of the 2000 United States Presidential election. This disruption has led to the current state of political unrest in this country. He's holed up in a chalet on a private lake. Your mission would be to apprehend him.

"What's his name?"

Hanging Chad.

And that's another story for another time…

FOR THE LOVE OF THE GAME

Blackie loved the game, and the game loved Blackie. Deep in the core of his being, *he knew* that tonight would be the catalyst for a metamorphosis; a moment of unparalleled transcendence in this sporting institution. It would begin with elation, and end in awe, with him standing under those big lights and everyone chanting his name.

BLACKIE! BLACKIE! BLACKIE!

The All-Star mastered the game long ago. From the batter's box to the pitcher's mound, around the bases and back again. The people sitting in the stands knew it, too. Each seat in the ballpark cost its occupant a cool twenty-five grand, tickets worth every penny to the spectators shelling out the dough. They came to see the biggest star player the sport had ever known, none other than number thirteen himself. The undisputed king of the homerun derby.

Blackie Sanchez.

He gripped the rail of the dugout with white knuckles

and watched the stadium's crowd from within the shadow of the roof. He could feel the energy of the spectators fill him with anticipation. The contest would soon begin and he was ready to deliver what they came for.

After the National Anthem, a flyover by the Air Force's drones brought a rousing cheer from the attendees. A fireworks display followed this up, just to make sure the crowd was ready for the contest to begin. When the familiar MLDBB theme music hit on the pipe organ, the seats grew wild with frenzied fans waiting for the annual All-Star Homerun Derby to begin.

"First," the announcer's voice bounced through the stadium as she called out each of the nine participants, one by one, "let me introduce tonight's pitcher. From the New York Warriors, number nine, Manny Valdez Aurelio Lopez Montoya Rodriguez, *Theee* Third! *Rodriguezzz!*"

The crowd popped hard for the MLDBB veteran. So did Blackie. He loved hitting off Rodriguez, the first, second, or third, it didn't matter. Tonight was sure to be a breeze, he reminded himself. This calmed his nerves some and allowed him to relax.

"And squatting behind the batter's box tonight, the catcher! From the Toronto Kaiju, number seven, Gaetano Pizzi! Pizzi!" Blackie noticed the catcher's rubberized uniform squeaked as he ran by. It reminded him of sneakers on a basketball court, when people still played those games. Now things were… different. The loudspeaker squawked and the announcer voice came back to life.

"And now your starting lineup! He's the anchorman for the Detroit Methheads, number seven, Tipper Longfield! Longfield! Next up, from the Los Angeles Crips, number sixty, Sydney Blackburn! Blackburn! The league MVP, from the Pittsburgh Zombies, number eleven, Dick Schlonghung! Schlonghung!"

Schlonghung's die-hard fans in the seats fisted the air. He could appreciate their enthusiasm. Blackie knew everyone loved Dick.

"Flying in from tomorrow, our Australian representative from the Melbourne Poppers, number three, Dingo Pagano! Pagano! He's spicy, the Designated Hitter for the Florida Men, number sixty-nine, Pepper Hyde! Hyde! He's the king of the Ground Rule Double, from the Salt Lake City Latterday Saints, number fifteen, Chick Singleton! Singleton! Next up is a man who needs no introduction, but we'll give him one anyway, the former three-time home run derby champion, from the New Jersey Diners, number two, Mando The Hammer Rosamilia!"

That's right, you're number two, Blackie thought, and smiled.

The names were barely recognizable in the echoing chaos, but no one cared, particularly Blackie. He knew he would be called out last. The slugger pinched a nostril and blew a snot rocket out of the other, waiting for his name to come through the speakers.

"We're getting near the end of the line up folks. Batting next, from your World Champion Minnesota Woodchippers, give it up for the dark horse of the competition, number twenty-three, Buckner Johnson! Johnson!"

Blackie spit out a wad of phlegm. It blasted into the sand and created an impact crater in the loose dirt. Buckner was lucky in the postseason. The rookie of the year last year, Buckner hit a few homers through the playoffs and World Series to get his team the pennant. Blackie knew there was no way in hell Buckner would place here, let alone win. This was the house Blackie built, and now he waited for his introduction, not as if he needed one.

"Finally, the man you've been waiting to see. The five-time! Five-time! Five-time! Five-time! Five-time MLDBB Home Run Derby champion, looking to make it six in a row. From the New England Lobster Rolls, let's give some love to number thirteen, *Reee-car-dohhh! Blackieee! Sannn-Chezzz!* Sanchez!"

Once it did, he hesitated another moment.

Blackie…

The anticipation built and a familiar, rumbling chorus grew in the stands.

Blackie. Blackie!

He sucked in the crowd's adoration with a deep breath, before running up the dugout steps, and onto the field. His fans, every person sitting in the stadium, popped at once for him. The roar cascaded into a rolling clap of thunder.

BLACKIE!

He raised his hands as he jogged to the infield to stand with his fellow competitors. They all slapped hands with him as he ran by, except for Mando Rosamilia. The Italian powerhouse from New Jersey dropped his arm, turned his head, and scratched his balls when Blackie reached him.

I see how it is, you fat fuck. I hope you choke on a pork roll, Blackie made a mental note of the transgression. Winning a sixth competition would be the best way to get him back. Sanchez no-sold Mando, pretending he didn't see it and instead attempted to double high-five with Buckner Johnson. The Woodchippers' first baseman missed, slapping at the air in between Blackie's hamfists. His fingertips caught the brim Blackie's cap, and sent it tumbling off his head.

How can you hit a ball over the wall if you can't even hit my hands? Blackie kept his thoughts to himself. Ever suave, he caught his cap on the back swing as he skipped to his spot at the end of the line up. They always saved the best for last, especially in exhibitions as grand as the All-Star home run derby. He joined the others as a unit, and bowed to the excited fans in attendance. The competitors ran off the field, passing by the outfielders and infielders from the MLDBB All-Star team who would be catching less than home run balls tonight.

Rodriguez walked straight to the mound. Pizzi went to home base. His rubberized uniform resembled a biohazard suit more than the typical jersey and tight pants of the other players on a team. He flipped on his face mask, then dropped the clear lexan shield over it. Sitting behind the batter's box was often messy business. The more PPE you wore, the better.

Clad in the candy striper uniform synonymous with ball girls, a cheerful young lady rolled out a cart with a bag of practice balls on it. The real deal was too valuable to use for warm-ups. Manny dug into the sack, pulled out a coconut sized ball, and tossed it in the air. He caught it in his glove, and stood on the mound.

Guy squatted down and opened his glove. Manny wound up, and whipped the practice ball underhand. It arched in the air at ninety mile an hour, before slapping into Pizzi's waiting glove. The catcher stood and threw the ball back. The duo repeated this process until Tipper Longfield decided he was done swinging donuts in the on deck circle. Blackie hated this procrastination bullshit.

Get on with it, already. He thought. Blackie wanted nothing more than to do his duty and get on with the celebration party.

The Detroit lefty took his time walking over to the plate. A hush fell over the crowd as he stepped into the batter's box. He held his pine bat with two gloved hands, and waited for the first pitch.

On the pitching mound, Manny Rodriguez waited, too, for the regulation balls. The ball girl pushed her cart as fast as she could from the sidelines back to the mound. An organ played a countdown of notes, building to a crescendo, bringing the crowd to life, and they cheered the ball girl on.

Blackie's irritation grew until Rodriguez took the bag of balls out of the ice basin, and the candy striper ran off with the cart, back to the sidelines. Regulation balls were always chilled. It allowed for fewer foul hits. Pizzi kneeled back behind Longfield, and Rodriguez, holding the ball inside his glove, waited for the catcher to nod—giving him the signal to release the first pitch.

"You better make it count," Blackie whispered, and focused his attention on the batter and catcher at home plate. Guy made a peace sign, indicating a fast ball pitch, and gave the signal to let it go. Each pitch he made with a regulation ball took a good eight or nine months to gestate and five grand. Rodriguez grasped the ball by the head, and wound up. His right arm made a full hundred and eighty degree arc before he released.

The ball, yeah, right. It's just a ball, Blackie reminded himself. It's all you could do. The masses asked for it, so they got it. Who was Blackie to question them? After all, they made him rich for hitting the ball as hard and as far as he could.

The ball tumbled through the air at around ninety miles an hour, its arms and legs spindling. The head, which carried the most weight also gave momentum to the pitch, like the tip of a badminton birdie. The ball went right to Longfield's bat.

The lefty, anticipating the ball's trajectory, got it right. He swung with all his might and the pine connected with the flesh of the ball. A bone shattering crack filled the stadium and the crowd erupted in awe. Bits of brain, cranial matter, bone, and coagulated blood rained on Manny as the ball flew over his head. It looked like someone sprinkled him with rainbow sprinkles in all the wrong colors.

Blackie winced. He bet Manny wished he was wearing Guy's rubberized catcher's uniform.

That shit is gonna be a bitch to wash out of his hair, the defending champ shrugged his shoulders, *oh well.*

The ball fell short and into the waiting glove of the centerfielder. The umpire behind Pizzi declared Tipper Longfield OUT! He jogged off the field to a round of jeers from the crowd.

It's a homerun derby, what did you expect them to do if you hit a fly out to center on the first pitch? Blackie didn't tell Tipper. It wasn't worth the time to acknowledge him, or the next batter.

Sydney Blackburn. The LA Crip fouled his first ball, clipping off a leg. Once an MLDBB ball has been dismembered, it doesn't have the same aerodynamic qualities it once possessed. The follow up pitches resulted in three more fouls, and three more amputations.

The fifth time might have been a charm, if Blackburn hadn't line driven the ball into the shortstop, Zucky Bergdiggler. Number Fifteen wasn't ready for it, and the ball splattered on his chest, knocking him to the ground. A giant, black stain covered the front of his uniform, but enough of the ball saturated his glove for the ump to call Sydney out.

Pizzi wasn't any better off than Zucky. By the time Blackburn was done swinging for the fences, Guy was covered in little fingertips, toes, and a tacky goo best described as *onlylordknowswhat*.

The crowd chanted for Dick, and Schlonghung rose to the batter's box. He choked up on his bat and waited for the first pitch. On the mound, Rodriguez dug through the bag, looking for the right ball for the batter.

Back in the dugout, Blackie bet Rodriguez loved

nothing more than to pitch an out during the All-Star home run derby. Sanchez knew for the pitcher, an out was a homerun. With this logic, he'd already hit two 'out of the park' to start off the exhibition. Blackie knew the league MVP would change all of that. Dick never disappointed his fans.

Manny's pitch landed in Schlonhung's sweet spot. But unlike Tipper earlier, Dick slapped this ball in the face. The impact sent it careening through the air, and over the left field wall for the first homer of the night.

The crowd went crazy, all except the poor sons of bitches covered in bone shards and internal organs from a seven pound, eight and a half ounce regulation MLDBB ball. Those folks either vomited on the spot, or ran for the closest lavatory to expunge.

The Aussie, Dingo Pagano, was a day late when he popped one up and out. Pepper Hyde did some seeking when he came to bat, next. The Florida Men DH sent his second pitch into the bleachers to get on the leaderboard.

Then, as Chick Singleton was living up to his rep as the King of the Ground Rule Double, Mando waited on deck.

Staring at Blackie as he warmed up.

Six years before, an upstart Sanchez usurped The Hammer's reign as MLDBB's Homerun Derby Champion. For the last few weeks, the lead in stories across sporting news made it no secret Mando planned on taking back his title. He stepped over to the batter's box the moment Chick pulled off the expected and left a giant grease stain on the centerfield wall.

The Hammer, his eyes ice and cold, waited for his pitch. Blackie wished for Manny to beam the son of a bitch in the face with the ball, but he couldn't be that lucky.

The pitch came, and Mando swung. His bat smacked into the ball, reversing its motion. It flew high, spinning and building speed as gravity pulled it back down, over the center field wall, and into the bleachers.

The occupants of the impact zone were given ample time to move, and they didn't hesitate to hustle out of the way. The ball hit the aluminum seats and turned into something resembling strawberry jam, covering the immediate vicinity in a pinkish ichor.

The attendees popped and drowned out the announcer, who declared The Hammer as the current leader. Mando dropped his bat and raised his hands over head. He pointed to the stands, and to the dugout.

Right at the five-time champ.

Sanchez didn't care, he no-sold Rosamilia's show of bravado, the same way he ignored him on the field earlier. It was his turn to go to the on deck circle, and Blackie didn't care. He stayed put.

You want me to bring it? Blackie thought to himself. *Oh, I'm going to bring it, don't you worry.*

Blackie could see Buckner Johnson didn't care about him or Mando. The first baseman left the on deck circle with a scowling disposition and one apparent mission: to prove himself. Blackie was certain Buckner would prove himself out in three strikes. Sanchez counted along with the umpire as he called Rodriquez's first pitch, "Strike one!"

"Strike two!" Followed the second pitch. The ball pinwheeled past Buckner's swinging bat into Pizzi's waiting glove like the first pitch. Buckner stepped back from the batter's box, kicked the dirt off his cleats, and took a breather.

Blackie smiled from the dugout's shade. In his mind he pictured Buckner hitting a line drive to the waiting arms of the left fielder, followed by the umpire calling Buckner out, leaving one contestant remaining.

Not all of this pipe dream came true. There would, indeed, be one contestant remaining. But Buckner wouldn't strike out.

Rodriguez wound up and lobbed the ball. It pinwheeled and hung in the air forever, giving Bucker an opportunity to zero in. He swung the bat and connected with his target.

The crowd went silent.

They all watched while the ball soared over the centerfield wall, past the seats, and into the LED scoreboard. The screen shattered and exploded. A fury of sparks, glass shards, and liquified remains showered the fans in the stands below the scoreboard.

"You've got to be fucking kidding me," Blackie said aloud, his jaw agape. Across the dugout, he saw Mando throw his hat.

A low rumble grew from the seats.

Buckner…

It got louder with each passing moment.

Buckner.

The spectators went crazy.

BUCKNER!

Blackie couldn't believe his ears. These were *his* fans, and they were chanting the lucky asshat's name.

Buckner! Buckner! Buckner!

This isn't happening, Blackie told himself. This was Blackie's game, his contest to win, not lose, and some punk from Minnesota wasn't going to be the one to do it.

The defending champ's limbs shook, his heart raced, and his palms grew moist with sweat. He took a deep breath, trying to compose himself before he walked to the plate.

You can do this, Blackie, he told himself, *No–you WILL do this!*

The crowd's adoration of Buckner diminished as Blackie finally stepped out of the dugout and onto the field.

Blackie.

The attendees chanted his name in earnest.

Blackie!

Sanchez stretched with his bat on the way to home plate, exorcising the last of the nerves Buckner set on edge. When he arrived, Blackie couldn't hear himself think thanks to his adoring fans in the seats. They forgot all about the Woodchipper's star player and his pyrotechnic display.

BLACKIE!

Manny retrieved the last ball from the bag, the one he saved all night for Blackie Sanchez. He readied it, twisting the waxy head in his hand until he was certain of the grip.

Buckner and Mando watched from the sidelines, neither bothering to sit back down. They obviously wanted to watch their nemesis either strike out or fall short from a front row seat.

The Hammer will go home disappointed, Blackie assured himself, *Buckner, that lucky little punk, will go home disappointed.*

Pizzi called for a slider. Manny Rodriguez agreed, wound up, and released the ball.

It's just a ball, Blackie, he told himself one more time as the infant—*No! It's a ball!*—pinwheeled through the air. It swerved in its trajectory, going wild. Blackie watched the arms and legs flail as the ball flew over their heads and crashed into the netting behind home plate. Rodriguez shook his head in disbelief at the wild pitch. Pizzi ran back and retrieved it as the ball slid, head first, down the netting.

I thought I was off, shit, Blackie thought. He spit another wad of phlegm into the dirt, cocked his head, and rolled his shoulders. The calm he knew returned. He turned to stare down the pitcher, and readied the bat to swing. Rodriguez wound up and released.

This time the ball—*It's a only a ball and this is only a game,* Blackie reminded himself—was dead on, and so was Blackie Sanchez. The defending champ swung his bat as hard as he could. The pine connected squarely on the fleshy head of the ball, and sent it into orbit.

A hush fell across the attendees and players alike.

The infant cadaver flew high above the players on the field. It gained altitude as it traveled, the outstretched, flailing arms and legs catching the wind, and giving it flight. Blackie swore he saw the little corpse doubling fisting the bird at the audience below with its little hands, sending them off with a proper "Fuck you." It went higher, and further; soaring above the bleachers and shattered scoreboard.

Until the ball disappeared over the stadium's wall.

Blackie dropped the bat. He pointed to deep center field with one arm and gave Buckner a finger of his own with the other. The fans had witnessed history, of this the defending champ was certain, and the Woodchipper's star learned number one was spelled *t–h–i–r–t–e–e–n*.

Outside the stadium in the parking lot, the din of crashing glass could be heard. A car alarm echoed in response, signaling the fans in the seats to come back to life.

Blackie! Blackie! Blackie! Their chanting resonated, showing their love. Blackie snorted a chuckle, knowing some poor soul would leave this contest to discover a surprise covering their vehicle. They'd probably make a good payday selling it on an auction site, if there was enough left of the ball to scrape up.

Blackie! Blackie! Blackie!

Sanchez saw the tears well in Buckner's eyes before the Woodchipper's first baseman disappeared into the locker room. The Hammer snorted, ignored Blackie's taunts, shook his head and turned away. Sanchez knew he'd see Rosamilia again, and Buckner, too, sooner than later. The next Major League Dead Baby-Ball All-Star homerun derby was only a year away.

Blackie! Blackie! Blackie!

Fireworks erupted and the crowd went wild. The

announcer declared Blackie Sanchez, number thirteen, "the six-time, six-time, six-time, six-time, six-time, six-time champion!" The fans counted along, their roar louder with each progressing chat. They loved him, and number thirteen loved each and every one of them.

Blackie! Blackie! Blackie!

Who says dead babies aren't any fun? Blackie Sanchez thought as he basked in the glory of his personal dynasty, *they're a blast.*

Right out of the park.

ACKNOWLEDGMENTS

Before I get into the meat and potatoes of this book, a huge thanks to Todd Keisling for doing the interior formatting. I typically do this myself, but Todd's a pro and he really made this look sharp inside. And I can't forget my new artist collaborator, Miguel Amaro-Santiago, whose pencils and inks on the interior plate of this volume stand out.

Most of the stories compiled within this volume were written during one of the most tumultuous times in recent history. Some were written for open calls, and others for workshops or writing prompts. A couple I wrote for the hell of it. These are not "feel good" stories, though some of them have what can only be called "inappropriate" humor. They will leave you wishing to hug a furry animal, lose yourself in an addiction, or stifle a laugh you feel guilty for finding. It's hard to imagine, leading up to the time I wrote these, I only wrote a little over a dozen pieces of fiction. Oh sure, I'd written hundreds of thousands of words as a journalist, but as a fiction writer, my output was sparse, until I decided to apply myself to the craft.

These tales are the bounty of this decision.

Part of this education was listening to podcasts by my future peers, and probably the most influential on me was John Urbancik's INK STAINS, a project wherein he wrote a story a day for a year. I took this advice, sought out a mentor, and entered workshop after workshop.

Lisa Vasquez and Garrett Cook are the hands-on teachers responsible for what you are about to read. Between Garrett's monthly writing workshops and Lisa's writing prompts, in the last seven years I've written an astounding amount of content, at least for myself.

Of the short stories I've written, ten of the most extreme I've put on paper are contained here. Some have seen multiple incarnations, with appearances in anthologies, previous collections, or as exclusive chapbooks. Are they good stories? I think so. They're fucked up, I know that much, as I've already noted. Some are bloody gore-fests, and a couple are a bit quieter—and much more disturbing—as a result. So if you came here for violence ridden depravity, shitty mothers & shittier fathers, broken taboos, and dead babies by the baker's dozen—*you're in luck.*

And yes, this rant has been your passive-aggressive trigger warning.

Happy nightmares!

Thomas R Clark
November 2023

Thomas R Clark is a two-time Splatterpunk Award Nominee (Best Novella, 2021 for BELLA'S BOYS and Best Short Story, 2022 for FIREFLIES & APPLE PIES). His most recent release, A PRAYER FROM THE DEAD, is available through St. Rooster Books. His journalism and entertainment critiques have appeared in *Rue Morgue, Stranger With Friction, House of Stitched Magazine, This Is Infamous,* and miscellaneous internet outlets. Tom lives in Central New York with his wife and their canine companions.

PRAISE FOR THOMAS R CLARK

SUMMERHOME

"If your greatest fears involve aging, infirmity, senile dementia, and a miserable, lonely, humiliating decline, then SummerHome is the book for you, because things could still get so, so much worse!" —Christine Morgan, author of *Lakehouse Infernal* and *Trench Mouth*

"Not since Lansdale's *Bubba Ho Tep* has a setting like this been used so perfectly. Clark knocks *SumerHome* out of the park with a blend of folk lore and modern horror." —Robert Ford, author of *Burner*

THE GOD PROVIDES

"Beginning with a series of gruesome murders, *The God Provides* spins the reader a grimly beautiful tale rooted in old world folklore and modern monster mythology." —Nikolas P. Robinson, author of *May Cause Ocular Bleeding*

"From a captivating opening to a thrilling ending, Clark

has crafted an engaging story that will keep you on edge months after you finish the final page." —Jason Pitts, writer/director of *Masquerade*

BELLA'S BOYS: A TALE OF COSMIC HORROR

"A real mindfuck. Anchors the reader into a very specific moment and place in time...and then proceeds to pull on all the threads of reality around it." —Michael Kingston, writer/creator of *Headlocked*

"Clark uses music to set the era and the mood, like a soundtrack to bring the story to life." —Colin Delaney, AEW, ECW, 2CW & WWE Superstar

GOOD BOY: A TALE OF SURVIVAL HORROR

"It's Watership Down by George Romero" —Brian Keene, author of *The Rising* & *The Complex*

"A really fine piece of writing. It pulled me right along and brought tears to my eyes at the end." —Mike Duke, author of the *Amalgam Series*

THE DEATH LIST

"*The Death List*, brings elements of the first wave slasher genre (think *Halloween, The Burning, Silent Rage*) and throws in some *Spinal Tap*-esque rock and roll drama, which is a bit comedic" —Walter Ball, *The Necrocasticon Podcast*

"A tale that has ample sarcasm, brutal terror, and dread." —*The Voracious Gnome Book Reviews*

"A Prayer from the Dead is a superbly crafted religious dystopian tale. Part Boondocks Saints and part The Crow, this cyberpunk thrill ride will keep you engrossed the entire time." —Ezekiel Kincaid, author of *The Adventures Of Johnny Walker–Demon Slayer*